THE COLD STOVE LEAGUE

The establishment of the Casabranca bar (modelled after Rick's Cafe Americain in the movie *Casablanca*) took all Michael Reade's life savings and was the fulfilment of a dream for him and his partner, Frank Driscoll. But when Reade arrives to join Driscoll in Praia da Giz on the lush Portuguese coast, he finds himself involved in the plottings of international financiers, a sinister secret society . . . and murder. The action of this fast moving, urbanely humorous thriller moves across continents to a shattering conclusion.

THE COLD STOVE LEAGUE

Thomas Boyle

ATLANTIC LARGE PRINT

Chivers Press, Bath, England.
John Curley & Associates Inc.,
South Yarmouth, Mass., USA.

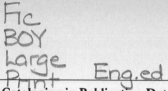

Library of Congress Cataloging in Publication Data

Boyle, Thomas, 1939–
  The Cold Stove League.

  (Atlantic large print)
  1. Large type books. I. Title.
[PS3552.O933C6 1988]   813'.54   88–18895
ISBN 1–55504–698–3 (pbk.: lg. print)

British Library Cataloguing in Publication Data

Boyle, Thomas *1939–*
The Cold Stove League
  I. Title
  813'.54 [F]

  ISBN 0–7451–9411–7

This Large Print edition is published by Chivers Press, England, and
John Curley & Associates, Inc, U.S.A. 1988

Published in the British Commonwealth by arrangement with
Robert Hale Ltd and in the U.S.A. and Canada
with Academy Chicago, Publishers

U.K. Hardback ISBN 0 7451 9411 7
U.S.A. Softback ISBN 1 55504 698 3

THE COLD STOVE LEAGUE

CHAPTER ONE

At seven o'clock on a gloomy June morning in 1972, a tall stranger entered a public house, The Cock, in London, near the River Thames and Billingsgate Market. The stranger was deeply tanned and wore a pale linen jacket and lime-green trousers. An expensive leather bag hung from a strap on his shoulder. He swaggered across the room to the bar, where he rested a moment, adjusting his paisley cravat and pulling at his drooping moustache, while his bloodshot, hawkish eye roved over the premises. He clutched a fistful of pound notes.

His presence was noted with interest by the other customers, who were almost all tradesmen and workers from the fish stalls at the market—the proximity of which dictated the pub's early licensing hours. Three diminutive porters, dressed in black and reeking of fish and Guinness, stood nearest the newcomer and regarded him with a mixture of alarm and amusement. At the corner of the bar stood a balding, youngish City type, who could be taking the last drink of the night or the first drink of the day. He paid no attention to the disruptive Yank, but contemplated instead the transient circles left on the dark wood surface by the glass of vodka-and-bitters which he raised intermittently to his lips.

'You got any bourbon, boy?'

The stranger was evidently an American: he drawled like a cowboy or a marine sergeant in a Hollywood film.

The landlord had no bourbon.

The stranger evinced disgust.

'Chivas Regal, then. A double. And double-time too. You get me?'

When it came, he threw back his head to gulp the scotch and slammed the glass onto the bar. The City man looked at him, shook his head and moved his chalk-striped bulk a few inches away, toward the wall.

The man began to sing in a loud *basso profundo*:

You can talk about your Clementine
Or even Rosalie
But the Yellow Rose of Texas
Is the only Rose for me.

He gestured for a refill. One of the porters wiped his hands on his black apron, and caught the American's eye.

'Y'all look like good ole boys,' he said expansively. 'Have one on me. And a refill for the dude, too . . . And yourself,' indicating the barman.

The drinks were poured in silence.

'Here's to the armed forces of our allied

2

nations,' the stranger said, and they all drank respectfully.

He set down his glass and drew his sleeve across his moustache. Strands of oily black hair had fallen across his forehead.

'I'm a Texan,' he announced. 'At Boot Camp I had to fight the damn Yankees first. Then I killed me some gooks at Pork Chop Hill. I wish we'd a made it to Suez; I coulda got me some A-rabs!'

He looked around the silent room. Suddenly he spat and slammed his hand down on the bar. 'At least, I could of got some A-rab poontang.' He laughed harshly. The other customers stirred nervously.

'Anyways, I been recalled. Re-*upped* is what I am. For a special mission.'

He turned his fingers into a pistol, and playfully strafed the room.

'Now,' he said, leaning forward on the bar, 'what kinda game do you all reckon I'm aimin' to bag hereabouts? What kinda chops do you figure I'm about to bust?'

The barman moved back from the bar. The porters shifted their weight uneasily again.

Suddenly the volatile American seemed to relax. He put his hands in his pockets and began to rock back and forth on his heels.

'I bet you fellas done time, too,' he said in a conversational tone. 'Howdyacallit? National Service? Right?'

One of the porters looked up from his mug

3

of black stout. He had a drifting eyeball.

'Not me, guv,' he said.

The Texan whirled suddenly on the City man.

'Where did you serve, old boy?' he asked.

The Englishman looked at him with bleary, disapproving eyes.

'Serve?' he said. 'What d'you mean, serve? I'm not in service.'

'National Service, sir,' the barman said in a low voice. 'That's what the gentleman is after.'

'National Service,' the City man echoed. He looked the Texan up and down with distaste. 'Actually,' he said, 'I don't see that it's any of your bloody business. So bugger off.'

The Texan appeared to find these remarks hilarious. He winked at the porters, and laughed until he choked. When his coughing subsided, he took a cigarette from the handkerchief pocket of his jacket with two fingers of his right hand. With his left hand he produced from another pocket a long black cigarette holder, fitted the cigarette into it, and inserted it between his teeth. He struck a match against the bar and then drew deeply on the cigarette, watched in fascinated silence by the barman and the porters.

Suddenly he whirled on the City man, who had relapsed back into an attitude of contemplation, and, poking his arm with a

4

long finger, blew a cloud of smoke into his face.

'Listen, son,' he said, laughing and coughing, 'some's soldiers and some ain't. That's what my daddy used to say.'

He brandished his long holder, flicking ash on the chalk-striped suit, and announced loudly, 'Old soldiers never die, you know. They just fade away. They . . . just . . . fa-a-a-de away . . . General MacArthur used to say that,' he said seriously to the City man.

'Time, gentlemen,' the barman said.

The Texan was startled.

'Time?' he said. 'What time?'

'Half-seven, sir.'

'By damn, I got 'to get movin'.'

He lowered his empty glass to the bar, gently this time, smiled widely at the company, peeled five one pound notes laboriously off his wad of bills, and dropped them on the bar. They amounted to triple what he owed.

'Well,' he said, in an approximation of a British accent, 'cheer-o, you chaps. I'm on my way to my last patrol.'

He walked to the door, turned, saluted the room smartly, did a brisk about-face, and goose-stepped off into the grey morning. Strains of a mangled whistling of the Colonel Bogey march drifted into The Cock.

There was a general shifting and settling after he left.

'Pissed to the ears,' one of the porters said.

'Not quite right,' said the one with the eyeball. He made a circling motion near his ear with his index finger.

'Bloody vulgar,' mumbled the City man. 'Damned offensive.'

Outside, the American was overtaken by a fit of coughing. He spat into the cobbled street and then impatiently shook the cigarette out of its holder, flinging it into the gutter where it landed with a damp hiss next to an unplucked headless chicken. He doubled over with coughing again and noticed he was standing in front of a sign that read 'Ikey Solomon Jellied Eels'.

Jellied eels and headless chickens. Suddenly his gorge rose. He drew several deep breaths and gradually the sensation passed. He saw again the bewildered, well-intentioned faces of the little limeys in the pub. They were good guys—the sort he would have liked to lead at Pork Chop Hill or Suez. If he had been to those places in the fifties, taking charge, risking death . . . instead of stuck in Tokyo next to a short-wave radio . . . He might not be alive now. But anyway he certainly wouldn't be in the mess he was in now.

He had never had any troops, he had none now, and he was never going to have any. He was alone, with a noose around his neck that he had helped to fashion himself; fifteen hundred miles away from a home that wasn't a home but a second-rate escape hatch at the end of the world. And now he had made everything worse by wasting his internal resources in an all-night booze-up—not to mention the possibility of blowing his cover.

At Lower Thames Street he turned up toward the bridge. He felt quite dizzy. What he needed was one last drink. He should have brought a bottle. But the bag was too heavy already; it was cutting into his shoulder. At the same time the weight of the pistol and the tapes and ropes gave him a feeling of security, and of purpose. He had to remember that he was not alone after all: there was Michael, and there was Georgia. He was doing this for them.

So what if he had made a bit of an ass of himself in that pub? Life was just a big act anyway, wasn't it? And he was entitled to a night on the town before combat. He was used to drinking and working. He was trained to handle both. He was fit for the job.

He felt revived, able to cast a cold eye on life's failings; he would fashion reality to suit himself. He wasn't tired any more, and he was really sober. Twenty-four hours without sleep was nothing to him. But he was a little cold. He was dressed for warm sunshine, not cold drizzle.

At the Monument he paused again, to orient himself. The river was behind him, junk scows rode the tide; the Union Jack flew from the Royal Exchange. The clock on the Ridgeway Teas building told him he had twenty minutes before his appointment. He removed a paper from his jacket and read the typewritten instructions for the last time, lingering over the attached glossy photograph, attempting to imprint the chinless, effete face indelibly on his memory. The guy would be a pushover. He put the papers away and hiked the bag onto his shoulder once more. Everything would be A-OK. This one was for Michael.

'Here's one for the Gipper,' he said loudly. At least three faces under bowler hats turned toward him. 'Pat O'Brien and Ronald Reagan,' he called after them. 'Fighting Irish.'

He strode up King William Street, on his last patrol. When he reached the Bank Circus, fed by seven streets, he realized he had gone too far and turned off into Lombard Street, walking close to the walls and attempting to blend into the grey stonework. Lloyds Bank was at the corner of Lombard Street and Pope's Head Lane.

The man whose picture was stapled to the instructions came suddenly around the corner. He wore spectacles with black plastic frames and a rumpled tweed suit. He was hatless; straw-coloured hair was brushed limply across his balding pate.

'Mr Eliot, I presume,' he said, stiffly. 'I am Ian Anderson,' They shook hands, the American apologizing for the necessity of so early a meeting. He spoke softly and his Texas drawl was gone.

'No bother at all, sir,' Anderson said. 'I am always here to join St Mary Woolnoth as she strikes eight.'

As if on cue, the church bells began to toll, a peculiarly flat, dead sound. Anderson led Eliot into one lane and another, and soon they were in a maze of narrow alleys, buried among the open avenues of the City. Anderson turned into a deepset doorway. 'My own private entrance,' he said. 'It leads directly to my domain, and it simplifies the problem of security.' He turned some keys, and they were in a small office, windowless and indirectly lighted; they moved into a large room, one wall of which was lined with telex machines and computers. A tiny middle-aged man was hunched over the keyboard of one of the telexes.

'Good morning, Lambourne,' Anderson said. Lambourne did not look up.

'Lambourne is my night staff,' Anderson said. He pointed to the machines. 'And this is what I like to think of as my laboratory. I am a scientist, Mr Eliot, not a capitalist, in spite of my place of employment.'

The American spoke, with a cutting edge to his deep voice.

'Mr Anderson, may I ask how you knew that I was the person you were supposed to meet?'

'Oh, now, Mr Eliot . . . may I call you Tom? . . . I know Americans are informal. Only an American would stand on Lombard Street at eight a.m. dressed like that . . . California clothes?' He turned to the telex machines. 'Let me explain my innovation . . .'

The American reached into his bag, removed the pistol and struck downward, hard, at the back of Anderson's head. The night man turned toward him, half rising, and he raised the pistol again, and hit him too, across the side of the head. He swung the bag off his shoulder, took out the ropes and cloth and bound and gagged the two men.

It was hard work. Grunting and wet with perspiration, he dragged each in turn to a tiny lavatory and shoved them in, helter-skelter. There was no time for polite positioning. Then he pulled two containers of electro-magnetic tape from his bag, and went to work on the machines.

At the dead stroke of nine, the tall American made his way through the overflowing circus of the Bank of England. He ducked down the stairs into the Underground and dropped the shredded remains of the instructions and the photograph into a trash receptacle. After a

10

few minutes of staring at the maps of the Underground system on the wall, he found himself confused, and ascended to the street where he hailed a cab and directed the driver to take him to the West End Air Terminal in the Cromwell Road.

They made their way west against the flow of the rush-hour traffic, passing a sign commemorating the site of Newgate Prison. When they stopped for a red light on a busy corner of The Strand, Tom Eliot stepped quickly out of the cab and dropped the pistol in its paper bag into the open back of a garbage truck. When the light changed he was back in the cab, comfortable in his seat, breathing a sigh of relief. An old soldier, he thought, knows when a job has been well done.

CHAPTER TWO

From a desk five and one half storeys above the Bahnhofstrasse, the maximum legal height of buildings in Zurich, Hans Hauptmann manipulated the foreign exchange market through the mouthpieces of two gleaming white telephones. His male secretary, listening in on extensions, transcribed the conversations in shorthand on a leather-bound note pad: on one phone

Hauptmann persuaded an American client that the French franc was basically unstable, especially in the light of its chronic need for outside support from the German commercial banks; into the other phone he barked orders to one of his Lugano agents to hold fast to his net-long position in dollars.

After one particularly long-winded exchange of jargon, in which he seemed to play simultaneously the roles of speaker, auditor and Greek chorus, Hauptmann pushed his chair back from his desk, crossed his palms across his torso, and breathed deeply.

'The donkeys at Fidelity Bank continue to sell dollars short, Gustave,' he said. 'However, we shall continue to hold the line.'

Gustave recognized, from his employer's posture, and from the summary of the day's events, that he was being politely dismissed. He buttoned his dark suit jacket, gathered his notebook and pencils, and quietly left. Hauptmann remained motionless in his ruminative attitude until he heard the closing of the outer office door. Then he sat up, with renewed alertness.

He opened his gold watch and ascertained that it was indeed five o'clock. He had the office to himself. His sister would not expect him home until seven. Rising, he left his office and entered a long, empty corridor. The third door on the left led into the research department of his organization; it was a commodious room with a view of the lakefront, and held a ticker tape, a telex machine, and the desks of the five clerks he employed to sift the tons of information available daily to the financial world.

Stacked on one of the desks were the ten late editions of afternoon newspapers, Swiss and foreign, to which his company subscribed. He thumbed hurriedly through them, biting his lower lip, until he found what he was looking for. The article was on page five:

PUZZLING BREAK-IN AT LONDON BANK

Authorities expressed mystification as to the motivation of a man who entered the Foreign Exchange Communications Centre of Lloyds Bank under false pretences this morning, and assaulted the Director of Operations and a member of the night staff.

Scotland Yard spokesman J. Burnham said that the Director, I. Anderson, had arrived at the office early for an appointment with a man representing himself as the agent of an American investment house. On gaining access to Anderson's office, the man knocked the two Lloyds' employees unconscious, and imprisoned them, bound and gagged, in another room, where they were discovered upon the arrival of the rest of the staff at 9 a.m.

Burnham declares himself unable to fathom the purpose of the attack, since the bank's equipment was unharmed and, thus far, nothing has been discovered to be missing.

Sources close to the banking company speculate that the intruder may have thought he had gained access to a part of the bank where cash was kept and that, discovering his mistake, he had fled.

Mr Anderson expressed concern about the two hour delay in operations which resulted from the assault, especially in light of the heavy trading caused by the recent 'floating' of the pound.

Hauptmann exhaled slowly; his thin lips widened into a smile. He sank into a chair, and looked out the window at the steamers on the blue Zurichsee, the white Alps in the distance. He could see the fountain in the Buerkliplatz and the giant California sequoia tree in the garden of the Bar au Lac Hotel. On the Quai Guisan, across the Platz, a young woman with a scarf over her hair, and wearing a rain slicker, was attempting to feed a perambulant swan. Tentatively she proffered the biscuit, or whatever it was. The bird's head darted back like a cobra and shot forward viciously toward her hand. She jumped back, and the swan gobbled the biscuit from the ground. Hauptmann smiled again, with deep pleasure, and settled farther into his chair.

He wondered how much the Crédit Suisse and the other banks knew. He folded the paper neatly and picked up a telephone.

It was noisy in the restaurant on the other end of the line, and it took some time to page Zwingli. While he stared at the magnificent gardens of the *quais* at the foot of the world's richest street, Hauptmann heard empty cocktail chatter and the barbarous thud of American music from the disco bar. With distaste he pictured the air-conditioned room, with its Las Vegas decor, filled with the faceless generation of computerized bankers.

'Walter Zwingli here.'

'Hauptmann.'

'Oh, mein Herr!' Zwingli's tone of cosmopolitan arrogance was muted at once. Such deference was of course natural, and expected, from a person likc Zwingli to the country's leading independent Foreign Exchange broker, no matter how many rumours of a break-up were spreading around. 'I am at your service, Herr Hauptmann.'

'Have you heard anything about the curious entry into Lloyds?' Hauptmann asked, in the guttural dialect of their home canton.

'Oh, yes sir,' Zwingli responded, also in dialect. 'It is the talk of the Paradeplatz: a bank robber goes in the wrong door and finds a lot of machines . . . It's pretty funny . . .'

'It is no joke,' Hauptmann said. 'Does it not seem curious to you that a person who planned such an operation would not know the difference between a bank vault and a telex centre? Do you know anything that is not in the papers?'

'Well, certainly. That is my speciality. Please hold. I have some notes.'

Hauptmann stood up, and shifted the phone to his other ear. He sat on the corner of the desk. The Alps were receding into haze. The tiny steamers had begun to pitch on the choppy waters of the lake. Zwingli returned to the line with a clatter, and spoke again in cosmopolitan accents:

'I have two somewhat contradictory items.'

Hauptmann sighed. Zwingli loved to indulge himself in complex prefaces. 'Please go on. I'm sure I'll understand.'

'First, the man who perpetrated the break-in appears to have been traced, at least partially.'

Zwingli paused impressively, and then went on.

'He seems to have been carousing through the night in various London *boîtes*. A London paper printed Anderson's description of the man's dress and a publican has turned up who remembers seeing him early in the morning near the bank. Also he had a *contretemps* at midnight with the manager of a night club. Both witnesses say he was drinking heavily and his behaviour was eccentric. He was alternately jovial and bellicose; he claimed to be a war hero.'

Ice cubes rattled over the line. Hauptmann chewed his lip.

'Perhaps,' Zwingli said, 'perhaps he wanted to be caught, you know? Prevented from committing the crime. Or he was only a hired-hand—an amateur; but—'

'Now,' Hauptmann said, 'was there something else?'

Zwingli lowered his voice. 'This may not be at all related to the war hero, Herr Direktor . . .'

'Let me decide that, Walter.'

Zwingli drew an audible breath and continued:

'There is a special meeting tomorrow at Crédit Suisse. Representatives from the Bankers' Association and the Vorot have been called in. And Crédit Suisse has been on the phone to London all day—to Lloyds in fact . . .' He dropped his voice confidentially. 'I have pursued the answer to the first question which entered my mind when I heard of this . . .'

17

'Whether Scotland Yard or Interpol or our police have been notified of the meeting?'

'Mein Herr, you are a step ahead of everyone.'

'Never mind the flattery, Walter. What is the answer?'

'The answer is "no",' Zwingli replied, smugly. 'There appear to be serious consequences here in Zurich of the London break-in . . .'

'The idiots on the Paradeplatz are still more concerned with the inviolability of their profession than with the protection of their investments. So. They have chosen to handle the situation without the police.'

'Exactly.'

'Very good, Walter. I shall be at home this evening.'

Hauptmann hung up and returned to his office. He checked his watch again. The sun was dipping behind the flat stone horizon across the Bahnhofstrasse. The leaves of the silver lime trees were floating in the breeze from the lake. Taking a Cuban cigar from the humidor on his desk, he clipped the end, and lighted it with a table lighter made of marble. He leaned back and suddenly the flesh around his dark eyes crinkled, and his laughter resounded loudly in the empty room. He sat for a moment, and flicked the first cigar ash deliberately onto the carpet. Then he rose swiftly and returned to the communications office.

He seated himself at the telex, with the cigar smoking in an ashtray at his side. First he inserted his index finger in the telephone dial mounted on the face of the machine and twisted off the digits for the World Communications Corporation carrier from Zurich: 1–0–9. Then, more tentatively, he typed with one finger 8–3–2, the telex area code for Portugal. Waiting for the answer-back code confirming his open line, he relaxed, and puffed on the cigar.

When he received the go-ahead sign, he replaced the cigar in the ashtray and pushed back the sleeves of his jacket, flexing his fingers before the keyboard. Using two fingers, he repeated the area code and the individual number in Portugal which he was attempting to reach: 8–3–2–4–6–5–9. The Portuguese answer-back came shortly: GIZCLUB, the letter code for the destination of his call.

He began to type in English, pausing to allow the carriage to lower and rattle back to the left-hand margin. He hit two keys, 'FIGS' and 'D'. Then:

THIS IS HANS. WHO ARE YOU?

He hit 'FIGS D' again to signal for response. The machine typed:

HELLO HANS. COLD STOVE HERE.

Hauptmann typed:

LOCAL REACTION TO OPERATION AS EXPECTED.

He paused, frowning, and then went on:

UNFORTUNATE REPORT OF DISCIPLINARY PROBLEM WITH TECHNICAL STAFF. HEAVY DRINKING. PUBLIC DISPLAY IN VICINITY OF OPERATIONAL AREA. BAD FOR CORPORATE IMAGE.

The machine replied:

STAFF HAS NOT YET BEEN DEBRIEFED. PERHAPS A MISTAKE. IF NOT IT WILL NOT HAPPEN AGAIN.

Hauptmann thought this over, and then he returned two stubby fingers to the keys.

ARE THERE RESULTS YOUR END?

The message from Portugal came quickly:

TARGET ONE COMPLETE SUCCESS. TARGET TWO ABORTED. NO

DIFFICULTY ANTICIPATED IN COMMENCEMENT OF NEXT PHASE.

Hauptmann responded:

THIS PHASE DEMANDS TIGHTEST ORGANIZATION. ANTICS ARE INTOLERABLE.

The Portuguese correspondent appeared to pause. Then the machine typed rapidly:

I AM IN PICTURE. NOT TO WORRY. WILL CALL TOMORROW AFTER DEBRIEFING. BIBI. 4659 GIZCLUB. TLX VIA WCC DIAL 109

The machine stopped. He stoked the cigar with deliberate puffs. Its tip glowed red against the pale blue walls of the room. A lone sail remained on the lake, which was calm again. The telex machine came alive again to tell him that his call to Portugal had begun at 1801 and had been concluded at 1815 hours. Barring traffic difficulties, he would be home on the north shore of the lake by seven p.m. . . 1900 hours telex time. His sister had promised *Carbonnades à la Flamande* for dinner. She would be putting the bottle of Dole on ice now, though she would prefer him to drink beer, as her late husband had done. Her late husband had been an imbecile, whose life had been dictated by what other people said and thought. A fat Belgian fool whose heart gave out while he was cavorting on a tennis court. His sister was far better off now with him, and she was a housekeeper who did things as their mother had done things, the right way. His mother had always served a glass of Dole, watered and slightly chilled, with dinner. And so it would be tonight. He felt, reflecting on the day's events, a surge of power.

He ground out the cigar vigorously, rose, and stretched. It was June 14, 1972. A day to remember.

CHAPTER THREE

The descent from the *serra* was quick. The earth was red where the sea peeped over the last of the foothills. There were shantytowns in which motorbikes competed with donkey carts. On thc sidc roads ubiquitous soldiers trudged in clouds of dust.

Michael Reade downshifted, and accelerated the rented Volkswagen out of the hairpin curve and around a dilapidated van with Portuguese plates. He was back on the downhill straightaway. Just above the tips of the forest of cork and pine, he saw orange roofs: another village, the last one before the coast.

He jerked the gearshift back up to third, easing the whine of the engine, and trod on the gas pedal. The little car rattled, dancing over the rough macadam. Reade's face flushed with exhilaration as the speedometer needle edged from one hundred to one hundred and ten to one hundred and fifteen kilometres per hour. He was literally hurtling toward the sea.

Suddenly he lifted his foot, braked slowly, and steadied his hands on the wheel, bringing the speed back under ninety. He exhaled, blinking. For a moment there he had almost gone out of control. It must be the combination, he thought, of jet lag and anxiety to reach a long-awaited destination. Certainly he could wait a few moments more, being so close now. On the other hand, perhaps he *should* go a little out of control, being now safely out of the New York rat-race.

'You *Ingles*?' asked the hitchhiker. These were the first words he had spoken since Reade had picked him up twenty miles to the north. He was only a boy, probably in his early teens, dark as an Arab, with flashing white teeth. He held a tiny yellow canary, which he shifted obsessively from one hand to the other and back to the breast pocket of his oversized orange shirt. He gazed at Reade with luminescent eyes.

23

'Not *Ingles*,' Reade said. 'American.'

'*Turisto?*'

'Not exactly. I own a restaurant in Praia da Giz.'

'The Casabranca?' the boy asked, eagerly.

'Yes,' Reade said, surprised. 'Are we so well known already?'

'I good friend of Senhor Frank. I live near. Sometimes I work Casabranca. Nice place.' He tapped Reade's arm significantly. 'Rich people. You married?'

'Not right now.'

The boy apparently squeezed the bird, which squeaked in protest. 'You know Senhora Ryan? Georgia Ryan?' He rolled his eyes.

'No. This is the first time I've come to Giz.'

'Well. She beautiful woman. Lots beautiful woman in Praia da Giz. *Ingles*, Swede, German, American. You like American girls?'

'I like all kinds of girls.'

'I have many girlfriends.'

'I'll bet you do.'

They had entered a village built on a river. At the last incline before the bridge, traffic was backed up. Reade put the car into neutral; it idled on the sunbaked cobblestones.

Suddenly the boy said, suspiciously:

'Hey. How you own Casabranca when Senhor Frank is *patrão?*'

'We're partners,' Reade said. He searched

24

for the Portuguese word. '*Socios*. I had to finish my work in New York, so Frank came over alone in December to open the place and get it going. Now I'm here for good. Understand?'

'What work in New York?'

Reade laughed. 'You ask a lot of questions,' he said.

'Senhor Frank was a famous actor in America! You actor too?'

'I've done some acting,' Reade said. It was not necessary to tell the kid that the only significant acting Frank had done in New York was the Humphrey Bogart imitation he had in the various saloons where he tended bar. 'Only I'm not as famous as Frank,' he added. 'Excuse me. Senhor Frank.'

The line of cars inched forward. The cause of the traffic jam was now visible: a trailer had stalled on the other side of the bridge over the rocky riverbed which bisected the white-washed village, and a funeral procession had been stopped because of it. Peasants wearing black armbands, darker than the dusty black of the garments, swarmed in the wake of a wagon attached to an undernourished donkey, with purple and pink plumes sprouting from its ears. On the wagon was a plywood coffin.

'*Muito* funerals in Portugal,' the hitchhiker said proudly. 'Lots of deads.'

Reade took off his sunglasses and rose a

little in his seat, squinting toward the bridge. A deputation of uniformed men had arrived there, their leader portentously surveying the assemblage. The plumed donkey defecated copiously, narrowly missing the feet of one of the officials. The boy caught Reade's eye and winked.

'Portugal has lots *policia* too. Senhor Frank say too much cops.' He spat out the window. 'No fuck around this place!'

Reade reached out and tousled the boy's coarse shock of hair. He thought to himself that the kid was a kind of good luck charm, a bright omen of a future of simple, direct spontaneity.

'Hey, Senhor. I check this out. Okay?'

The boy climbed out of the car without waiting for an answer and disappeared into the crowd on the bridge. He seemed to have picked up some of Frank's tough guy mannerisms. Reade sat back and stretched. Automatically, without at first realizing what he was doing, he adjusted the rear view mirror to look at himself, and began to comb his fair hair. It would soon need to be trimmed. Then he remembered that he didn't need to keep it carefully trimmed any more, really: he was no longer going to be a mannequin. And a mannequin was what he was, not an actor. His face had been his meal ticket, getting him TV commercials for hairspray and after-shave lotion. Posing. Not doing a job you would respect . . .

He put away the comb and made a face at himself in the mirror. He noticed two old peasant women staring at him through the windshield. One was pointing at him in disbelief: another crazy *yanqui* tourist. They turned away, clucking and shaking their heads.

That was a fitting conclusion to his career as a performer.

From now on, he would live, as Frank had put it, without a script. He smiled, contemplating an array of new anarchic identities, to be taken on as the mood struck him: resident host and *bon vivant* of the Casabranca; sailor, skindiver . . . That would give the bar a glamorous image . . . Image! He had come to the place the Portuguese call *O Fim do Mundo*, the end of the world, in order to find reality and get away from *images*.

He removed Frank's last letter from the map on the seat next to him, and read again:

The business is hanging together real good, as the sportscasters say. We've developed a clientele straight out of central casting, perfect for a sequel to the gang in Rick's Cafe Americain in *Casablanca*. We named it right. There was a bit of a problem looming on the corporate horizon, but I'm taking measures and everything will be *muito bom* when you get here on the 17th. I'll tell you all about it then.

Anyway it's all very poetic down here. You hairpin your way across some foothills called *Sierra de Espinhaco de Cão*—which freely translates as The Dog's Ass—and you soon find yourself contemplating the Invasion of the Hun at Lagos. Bear right there and drive a few miles further, following your eyes to the water. Giz sneaks up on you. There is a dip in the road, then a hedged curve, and suddenly you are in the middle of a cubist painting. Our gin joint lies at the foot of the corniche, facing the beach.

Reade told himself for the tenth time that the mention of trouble meant nothing—Frank clearly had everything well in hand. He'd be happily surprised to see Reade there, two days early, ready to contribute. There was no sense in waiting around for three days, when the shooting at the studio had finished early, on June 13th, so he had flown to Lisbon on the night of the 14th, the first flight he could get, rented the Volkswagen at the airport and driven straight down, without bothering to cable or call. Frank would probably be pleased as well as surprised—Reade was at last being spontaneous.

There was a tap on the window. The old women again. One of them carried a little girl who was dressed like a Christmas tree ornament in a long white gown and with a golden crown on her head. She clutched a bunch of wilted flowers in a rather grubby little hand and looked irritated. The second old woman pointed to the flowers and then gestured to Reade, holding out a gnarled hand with blackened fingernails, while the first one tried to coax the child into a friendlier demeanour. She succeeded with some difficulty: the little girl broke into a wide smile and imitated the crone, holding out her hand for money. The second woman seized the flowers and poked them in the window at Reade. They appeared to be irises. They were quite dead.

What should he do? The flowers were worthless; the people were needy. The new businessman in him was inclined to push aside the free spirit whose impulse was to hand them a fistful of escudos. He hesitated.

Then the little hitchhiker was back, angrily shooing away the beggars. What a relief. The first Portuguese dilemma had been solved with dispatch.

The boy got back into the car with an air of having performed a necessary task with efficiency. He pointed ahead.

'Now we go.'

The stalled car had been moved, the funeral party was progressing. Behind them the driver of a long silver Mercedes leaned on his horn. Traffic began to flow over the bridge.

The road had narrowed into a lane, paved and bounded by stone, beyond which were flat scrubby fields and undulating groves of olive and fig trees. Brown emaciated cattle grazed; here and there was a scrawny goat. The distant hills were dotted with sprawling villas.

Then they were above Giz: whitewashed stucco and orange chimneystone, and the sea striped by banners of shade from a few drifting clouds. The boy pointed to an even more narrow lane which ran off toward the hills.

'Here I get off.'

Reade pulled up, and they both got out. The still air was redolent with a sweetish exotic perfume.

'What's that smell?' Reade asked.

'Africa,' said the boy. His eyes brimmed with amusement. He pointed south to the sea, and held out his hand to Reade, who shook it gravely.

'How are you called?' the boy asked.

'Michael Reade.'

'You are now *Senhor Miguel da Casabranca.*'

Good. A new name for a new personality.

'Thank you. And how are *you* called?'

'Antonio Jose. Senhor Frank calls me Big Tony. *Ate logo*, Senhor Miguel,' the boy said, running into the path.

Reade stood in the sunshine, breathing in the spicy air, and watching the small figure scramble down the hill. Across the horizon, like a camel train on a green desert, a flotilla of fishing boats returned from the open sea. All this was his now.

He called after Big Tony: 'Senhor Frank and I are going to have a drink now, and we're going to toast you, the best guide on the Algarve!'

The boy stopped and turned. 'Senhor Frank not here. Gone.'

Reade stared at him. 'But where could he go?'

'Who knows? He always gone in middle of week.'

'Will they know at the Casabranca?'

'*Quinta-feira*. Thursday. Casabranca closed Tuesday, Wednesday, Thursday. Middle of week. Nobody there. Maybe ask Giz Bay Club.'

His good luck charm waved and disappeared into the scrubby vegetation.

Reade stood looking out to sea. This was odd news. The Casabranca was supposed to be open all day, every day. It was in the contract. The African breeze stirred his hair.

It was 10 a.m., June 15, 1972. It was going to be a day to remember.

CHAPTER FOUR

At about the same time that Reade was entering the environs of Praia da Giz, Hans Hauptmann was pacing the floor of his research department office, watching a morning storm gather over the Zurichsee. The telex buzzed, and Hauptmann lunged for it, elbowing the operator aside. The message was short.

When time and charges were posted he ripped the sheet from the machine and hurried back to his private office.

Alone, Hauptmann read the message carefully once, and then again. His face was expressionless.

PLEASED TO REPORT EMPLOYEE PROBLEM TERMINATED. PHASE TWO WILL BE COMPLETED BY MONDAY. SEE YOU COLD STOVE AS ARRANGED. DO NOT CONTACT ME BEFORE THEN, GIZCLUB. TLX VIA WCC DIAL 109.

He sat for a long while, thinking, and watching the summer lightning crack across the lake. Then he fell into a doze, and dreamt that he was a bishop in a chess game, cutting diagonally through pawns like butter.

CHAPTER FIVE

'Funnily enough,' the red-faced Englishman said, 'I asked myself the same question this very morning. Where *is* Frank Driscoll? He's a man of mystery, that chap.' He nodded at Michael Reade over his glass of gin and tonic.

Reade attempted to suppress the feeling of uneasiness which he had had ever since he had learned that Frank was away. There was little comfort to be had in looking at the Casabranca, which was just down the beach from the poolside bar of the Giz Bay Club. It looked just like the realtor's snapshot: a three-storey cube of white stucco with a terrace projecting onto the white windswept sand. But chairs were piled on tables on the empty terrace and the doors were locked. Well, at least the building was intact.

The Englishman plucked a slice of lime from his drink and popped it into his small mouth. 'Portimão,' he said, 'Albufeira, Faro? I wonder. Wherever he is, I reckon he's on a monumental booze-up. I think his partner is arriving in a couple of days. Old Frank's off on a last big tear, I expect.' His hair, grey or blond as it caught the light, turned up over his protruding ears, like wings.

The woman sitting next to the Englishman spoke to him in a deep whisky voice. 'Come on, Clive, you're going to give Frank a bad name.' She looked at Reade. 'You're not from the consulate, are you? Frank's away on business, we all know that.' She sipped white wine. 'In Lisbon,' she added. 'He told me that, while he was standing right where you are yesterday morning. Georgia was taking him to Portimão to catch the airport taxi to Faro.'

Reade breathed more easily. Of course Frank must have a good reason for closing in the middle of the week. He wasn't so loose that he would be that irresponsible—any more than Reade was compulsively organized. He rather resented Frank's apparently having given that impression to these people. True, he *seemed* loose but that was the façade he presented. There was that problem Frank had mentioned in the last letter. Government red tape probably; that was a way of life in Portugal. Relieved, Reade was able to look at the Giz Bay Club for the first time: the blue oval pool sparkling in the sun, the formal gardens around the main building, the flowering vines on the thatched walls and roofs of the outdoor dining alcoves. A young woman lay sunbathing on a low wall which separated the pool area from the beach. The top of her bikini was undone and her brown back and thighs glistened with oil.

Reade felt himself relaxing. Frank was away on business. Maybe he was having a few drinks as well, stoking up against the work load that was coming for the rest of the season. Frank was a drinker, but he was a drinker who took care of business. His success in running bars in New York was legendary. Reade reproached himself: his confidence in his partner should not have been shaken so easily.

The sun was shining. Portugal was as sensual and welcoming as he had thought it would be. He smiled at his two companions.

'I'm glad to hear that,' he said. 'Because I'm not from the consulate. I'm Frank's partner.'

The woman looked delighted; her light blue eyes lighted up in her brown, rather leathery face. 'How terrific that you're here! Michael, isn't it? Michael Reade. You're on TV. Frank has told us nothing but good things about you.' She raised her wine glass in a sort of toast. 'Clive, you should be ashamed. Clive's terrible: he was only joking about Frank, and about you. He's a great kidder.' She inserted a cigarette into a long black holder and watched the flame from her lighter steady before she lighted up.

Clive was not at all embarrassed. He was amused. His insignificant nose and small cupid's-bow mouth seemed to melt into the rest of his face as he emitted strangled cries of laughter. 'How bloody marvellous, old boy,' he said, when he came to himself. 'I gave you a hell of a fright, eh? Sorry. Of course I was joking about the pub-crawl. Frank's all business, you know. Made the whole thing up out of whole cloth, really.' He stirred his drink with a stubby finger. 'He'll be here tomorrow and open the bar bright and early, you mark my words. You've come a bit prematurely, haven't you?'

'I finished work a couple of days ahead of schedule. I thought I'd surprise Frank.'

The Englishman's features vanished again as he dissolved into laughter. 'Oh,' he said, 'he'll be surprised all right.'

'Frank loves to laugh,' the woman said. She sounded as though she were describing someone whom Reade had not met and whom she was most anxious for him to like. 'He'll get a real chuckle out of this.'

A babyfaced young man with longish grey hair spoke from the corner of the bar. 'Don't be so goddam sure of yourself, Lucy,' he said. His voice was American. 'Frank's laughing a lot less these days. His consciousness has been raised; he knows the people in this country are oppressed . . .'

'Please don't start on that again, Philip,' Lucy said. 'It's too early in the morning.' She said to Reade, 'Philip is one of those spoiled brats who have ruined America with their vulgar communism. Now, he's stirring up trouble here; it's too law-abiding for his taste.'

'At least I didn't come over here to get in bed with the PIDE,' the young man replied to her back. 'That's the secret service. Gestapo,' he said to Reade.

Lucy wrinkled her nose in distaste, whirled around suddenly and threw the last of her wine in Philip's general direction.

'Please!' cried Clive. 'Let's not be so boring. How about a toast, to the new *patrão* of the Casabranca.' After a pause, they all raised their glasses. 'I'm Clive Mowbray,' the Englishman said. 'Lucy is Lucy Luce, you remember her, the star of stage and screen . . .'

Reade did not remember her.

'I'm Philip Vandermint,' the grey-haired young man said.

'Scion of one of the lesser branches of the Maryland Vandermints,' Mowbray said. 'Frank calls him a card-carrying member of the Porsche Proletariat. Now what are you drinking? Bloody Mary. Right. Eduardo! Lucy, another Magos? . . .'

'Tell us about the States,' Lucy said. 'Are things as bad as they seem? Everyone trying to undermine the President. I left when they began fornicating on the lawns in La Jolla . . .'

'Tell us about the Red Sox-Yankee game yesterday,' Vandermint said, 'and then get your saloon open, so we don't have to rely on this neo-colonial dump.'

'Red Sox, 3–2. Yaz hit a homer in the ninth with two on.'

'Hey,' said Vandermint. 'Terrific.' He smiled for the first time. A copy of *Sports Illustrated* was on the bar in front of him.

The Bloody Mary was made from freshly squeezed tomato juice, and, drinking it, he felt his own juices begin to flow. What a group this was. Mowbray, with his red Colonel Blimp face; Lucy Luce, with a blonde pageboy and a black linen dress, looking like a refugee from a Hollywood back lot in 1946, and Vandermint in trunks and torn T-shirt, talking about revolution in a prep school accent, and drinking screwdrivers at 11 a.m. Frank was right: they were straight out of central casting.

Frank. What was the problem he was taking care of? Beyond the wall where the sunbather lay, the beach was becoming populated; people were putting down towels on the sand at discreet distances from one another. Blue and white *cabañas* stretched across the sand at the foot of the Casabranca's handsome terrace. A lovely prospect, a beautiful place to work and play. To hell with worrying about Frank.

His drinking companions were lavish with compliments about Frank and the Casabranca. Lucy Luce called him the last of the true American rugged individualists. Vandermint said that he and Frank shared a passion for baseball and a habit of drinking *medronho*, the local moonshine, with soldiers returned from combat in Angola. Mowbray had found Frank an appreciative audience for his repertoire of limericks, and recited Frank's favourite—about a man from Dundee who raped an ape in a tree.

The fishing boats bobbled to attendance near a stone ramp at the edge of the water. They were gaily coloured dories with cartoon faces painted on the prows. The first boat was being dragged up the ramp to be unloaded. Reade's hair ruffled in the light breeze and his second drink tasted even fresher than the first, if that were possible. He stopped listening to the conversation, which was once more about politics. He was no longer interested in the peace movement, people blowing up buildings, the war against racism deteriorating into the survival of the most corrupt, the summer of love becoming the summer of pills. He had come abroad in search of the simple life, and he seemed to have found it, apart from the petty hypocritical squabble going on around him.

Near the ramp a small crowd of women carrying net bags had gathered around a man in a black suit and broad-brimmed hat; he appeared to be auctioning off the fish. The fishermen distributed their catch in concentric circles around him. A few curious bathers stood behind the women.

'It's a ritual,' Mowbray said. 'Centuries old. Chap in black is the *cabo do mare*, an important person—commander of the sea, so to speak, beach politician, you know, and chief entrepreneur. Frank would say that he has a piece of the action on everything from *cabañas* to fish. You have to remember to treat him well. I should have thought actually there wouldn't be an auction today, because of the Levant, you know.'

'The Levant,' Reade said.

'Yes, the wind that blows from the east. It's a three-day storm, makes fishing dangerous, sometimes impossible. The bars were full of fishermen last night; they thought they wouldn't be going out today. But the weather broke, and they went out, a bit the worse for wear, just past midnight. The auction's three hours later than usual.' He chuckled over the rim of his glass. 'Some colossal *medronho* hangovers on those boats, I daresay.'

To Reade the dark muscular men who were unloading the boats seemed singularly fortunate, hangover or not. Their livelihood and their environment were integrated. He drifted into a fantasy about owning his own fishing boat, reading the sea and the sky, at one with nature . . .

'What about McGovern?' Vandermint said. 'D'you think he has a chance?'

Reade was grappling a giant tuna aboard a

wave-swept, blood-spattered deck. 'What?' he said.

'McGovern. Can he win the nomination?'

'Oh . . . I suppose . . .' He shrugged and flashed his most winning smile. The last thing he wanted to think about was the election.

'He wants to give everything away,' Lucy Luce was saying. 'Weak . . .'

'Oh, I suppose you prefer spending money to kill babies in Vietnam,' Vandermint said. 'And Angola.'

'Now, the Portuguese experience in Angola is complicated,' Mowbray said. 'You don't want to oversimplify. I mean, look at Kenya . . . And one must know the peculiar character of the Portuguese . . .'

Vandermint laughed loudly. 'That's something you have to learn about,' he said to Reade. 'When Frank gets back, ask him. Ask him what it's like to spend a winter in Giz. Ask him about playing a series on the road in the Cold Stove League.'

There was a pause. Then Lucy said that Africans would still be sitting in trees eating bananas if it hadn't been for imperialism.

Somebody screamed on the beach. The bar boy pointed toward the boats.

The auctioneer was shouting officiously at three fishermen on the last boat who were attempting to hoist a large bundle onto the sand. It was attached to a big hook and the fishermen were lowering it by slowly turning

41

a winch. When it lay on the sand, someone screamed again.

'Someone's drowned,' Lucy Luce said. The girl on the wall sat up. The bar boy bounded past them onto the beach.

Mowbray ran clumsily after him, and Reade followed, scrambling onto the hot sand. It was all like a scene from a movie . . .

As he reached the grouping of people, he kicked over an earthenware pot filled with squid. The slimy creatures began to ooze onto the sand, near a pile of eel-like silver fish, which in turn were not far from the body. It lay in a circle of unshaven, barefoot men, whose trousers were rolled up to their knees. The sea had pulled the dead man's clothing halfway off, and the pallor of his torso made a sickly contrast to his sun-tanned hands and face. His jacket and shirt were bunched up around his shoulders, and his lime-green trousers and his jockey briefs had been pulled down around his knees. On one foot was an ankle-high boot; on the other a water-logged black sock.

Reade could not speak. Fingers dug into his arm and he heard Mowbray saying, 'Oh, bloody hell. It's Frank.'

The sky was too bright; voices ebbed and flowed with the sea; the people on the beach strolled from three-dimensional figures to blue outlines etched in tile like the *azulejos* which decorated the façades of the

Casabranca and the Giz Bay Club.

When his vision steadied, Reade saw close up for the first time the evil-eyes which had been painted on the fishing boats to ward off the spirits of the deep.

CHAPTER SIX

On that same morning, in Zurich, three men were meeting in a conference room built beneath the pilasters and geraniums of the Bahnhofstrasse.

The host was Helmut Zeigler, who at only forty-three years of age was already Senior Vice-President of Crédit Suisse; he was rumoured to be the next head of the bank. He was visibly upset, and stood at the head of the polished walnut table, his chair pushed back.

'I will come to the point immediately,' he said. 'We seem to be the victims of an embarrassing theft. It is potentially more embarrassing than the Helga Hughes affair.'

Leon Brunardi, who sat on Zeigler's right, sighed gently. He was an old man, President of the Swiss Bankers' Association. Across from him was the third man, Rudolf Escher, a vigorous fifty-year old, a watch manufacturer who was acting director of the Vorot, the powerful Swiss association of commerce and industry.

'Perhaps,' Zeigler said, 'you read yesterday about the man who got into the telex centre of Lloyds Bank . . .'

'Yes, yes,' Escher said. He pulled out a cigar, and bit off the end. 'Stupid, it was stupid.'

'He didn't steal anything,' Brunardi said. 'The papers said . . . Did he?'

'But he did,' Zeigler said. 'He set a theft in motion, from Lloyds, from Crédit Suisse. But that's not so much the issue, *who* he stole from.' He pulled his seat forward and sank into it. 'The issue is—'

'Yes, of course,' Escher said impatiently. He chewed impatiently on the cigar. 'How did he get the confirmation codes?'

'Please do not be so irritable, Rudolf,' Zeigler said. 'I did not ask you here so you could upset me. I am upset enough.'

After a pause he continued: 'The man who broke into Lloyds managed to telex a large sum of money from Lloyds to an account in our bank. The telex was confirmed; somehow he had the codes.'

Brunardi took off his silver-framed glasses and began to clean them with a large white handkerchief.

'Unfortunately,' Zeigler said, 'the deposit included instructions to disperse the moneys immediately. To Athens, the Greek National Bank . . . *Aethniki Trapeza* . . . and Madrid, the *Banco Hispano-Americano* . . .' He paused

44

again.

'Those banks have the money,' Brunardi said. It was a question, not a statement. He held the handkerchief and the spectacles in his hands and looked at Zeigler.

'Well . . . Luckily the Greeks failed to acknowledge the telex promptly . . .'

'Typical,' Escher said. He swivelled the cigar in his mouth.

'. . . but in Madrid . . . the money was withdrawn almost immediately by a representative of the company to which it had been sent. By the time the Greeks got back to us, we were able to intervene, but the other deposit is gone.'

He stopped again, and poured himself some ice water from a heavy crystal pitcher. The two men watched him drink.

'Well?' Brunardi said. 'How much?'

'One half-million pounds sterling.'

Brunardi put on his glasses slowly, and put his handkerchief neatly into his suit jacket. 'Has there been any significant foreign exchange movement?'

Zeigler shook his head.

'Well, I understand the delicacy of this situation,' Escher said. 'We can't afford this kind of publicity. The banks, our banks, Swiss banks . . . Inept and vulnerable, that's how we'll look—inept and vulnerable. Maybe worse . . .'

'I know,' Zeigler said. He closed his eyes

and leaned back in his chair. 'I know.'

'Corrupt,' Escher said. 'Never mind inept. And the bad publicity, secret accounts . . . Mafia accounts . . .'

Brunardi interrupted him. 'Do the police know?'

Zeigler shook his head again, his eyes still closed. 'Not yet,' he said.

'And whose Crédit Suisse account was it passed through?'

'World Communications. Money was transferred from one World Communications account at Lloyds to their numbered account here . . .' He looked at a pad of paper on the table before him. '2238 . . . and it was to be dispersed immediately to these small accounts in Madrid and Athens, you see.'

'And in Madrid?' Brunardi asked softly.

'We have not yet been able to establish co-operation with the Madrid bank.' Zeigler said gloomily. 'And Lloyds . . . There is no problem there, they will share responsibility with us, but we must make an explanation to World Communications, they cannot be kept out of it.' He rubbed his eyes and sighed. 'They are one of our major clients.'

'This is terrible,' Escher said. He frowned heavily, and his eyes popped slightly. 'Can't we pretend the money was never credited to the account?' He dropped his voice. 'The records can be fixed . . .'

'Well,' Zeigler said, 'I think we may be

able to work something out. We want to avoid publicity . . . World Communications might feel much as we do . . .'

'Ah,' Brunardi said. 'No one wishes to wash dirty linen in public.'

'That's right,' Escher said. 'So . . . we ask WC for an alliance . . .'

'Precisely,' Zeigler said. 'We are a united front here, I can count on that . . .'

He looked from one to the other.

'And so . . . we must have an investigation, we must find out. This cannot be allowed to happen again. We ask WC for a trouble-shooter . . . They have one, I hear, an American. His name . . .' He consulted the pad again. 'Turner Cromwell. Not pleasant, but discreet, I hear. He has managed house-cleaning for World Communications for years. As you know, they have an unblemished reputation.'

'And he is not connected directly with Swiss agencies,' Brunardi said.

'Exactly,' Zeigler said. 'We have had a preliminary conversation with him.'

'It may be all right,' Escher said.

'One glance,' Zeigler said. 'One glance at the movements in the WC account would be fuel for three international commissions.'

'He can come to Geneva?' Brunardi asked.

'He prefers to meet us in France,' Zeigler said wryly. 'He wishes to talk at dinner there.'

47

CHAPTER SEVEN

Motes of dust danced in the afternoon sunlight which streamed through the casement windows of the *Camera Municipal* in Lagos.

In the far corner of the cavernous room the young civilian translator, who had introduced himself to Reade as Jose Francisco Maria Churchill y Silva, of Oporto, was talking on the telephone. Reade sat in a chair facing the desk where the police captain sat, in his green uniform, looking officiously at various documents—Reade's among them. From the street below came occasionally the crepitation of a motorbike.

Silva hung up the phone and came to the captain's desk. They spoke in rapid Portuguese. The captain pushed his chair back, and crossed his legs. His stomach bulged beneath his polished black belt. He looked at Reade for a moment, and then nodded to Silva, who perched on the corner of the desk, casual in his tennis shirt and wide wale corduroy trousers.

'Your story has been corroborated, Mr Reade,' Silva said, in a nasal approximation of a British public school accent. 'You were indeed aboard TAP Flight 5902, New York to Lisbon, during the time at which the medical examiner places Mr Driscoll's death.'

Reade did not relax. He had not been worrying about what flight he had been on; he had been trying to suppress the recurrently rising image of Frank's corpse, lying among the glistening creatures of the sea.

'Captain Batista asks that you forgive him for detaining you for such a time,' Silva went on smoothly. 'You understand, of course: you arrive unannounced, two days early. Within the hour of your arrival your business partner is deposited on the beach, recovered from the sea off Sagres . . . dead . . .'

'Do you know yet what happened?'

'We will have a full report tomorrow morning. Now we have learned that your friend was apparently last seen leaving the Bar Tubarão in Sagres at eleven last night. He was alone.'

'Sagres is twenty miles away, isn't it?' Reade said. He was thinking aloud. 'Frank didn't have a car. What was he doing there?'

Silva smiled at him, with large white teeth. He wore thick glasses with grey plastic frames. 'We thought perhaps you could shed some light on that, Senhor,' he said.

Reade shook his head. He stood up, and picked up his jacket. He longed to get to the Casabranca, where he could bathe and change his clothes. After that maybe he would be able to think better.

'Well,' he said, 'thank you for your

concern. I think I'd like to get back now.'

He moved toward the desk, and his eyes met Batista's. The policeman's gaze was intelligent, and for some reason, threatening. Reade felt an inexplicable jolt of fear. That was what they were trying to do: frighten him. Batista said something to Silva in a hoarse voice.

'I'm sorry,' Silva said. 'The captain requests that you sit down for a moment longer.'

'I'm really awfully tired . . .'

'We appreciate that. But . . . you are physically exonerated from responsibility for this death, of course. But we wish to talk about your situation as a business association of the deceased.'

'Surely that can wait . . .'

Batista barked suddenly in Portuguese. Reade lowered himself wearily into the chair. It would probably be wiser in the long run to co-operate with them. He did not know what his rights were as an American citizen in business here. Suspicion hung in the air; he had not had to deal with that ever before.

'Now, Mr Reade. Your relationship with Mr Driscoll . . . it was friendly?'

'We've been friends for ten years. After he came over here, he wrote me every two weeks. Yes, we were friends.'

'And the business. How is it to be disposed of, now that he is dead?'

'Disposed of?'

'Yes. Who stands to inherit his interest?'

'I see what you mean,' Reade said. He took a deep breath, to try and dispel his irritation. 'The licensed premises and the building itself belong to me, completely. Frank was my employee. We had an agreement that if everything went well he would become a full partner in the restaurant after two years. But the property would still belong entirely to me. Frank didn't own *anything* here.'

'You are saying that he was not a man of means, that he had no property?'

'He did not have a cent,' Reade said slowly and distinctly. 'I don't know how much more clearly I can put it. I don't know of any life insurance, I doubt if there is any. He had no family. There wasn't any reason even for him to have a will.' He leaned forward. 'Can't you see that I'm left holding the bag? I don't profit from his death; on the contrary. I have no experience as a bar keeper, I don't speak Portuguese. I relied on Frank for those things.'

'Senhor Driscoll was fluent in Portuguese?'

'Well . . . he took a Berlitz course in New York. And he has been living here for six months.'

'The business was successful?'

Could these questions have something to do with a liquor licence? Maybe that was the problem Frank was trying to deal with, something about the licence.

'Frank indicated that we were breaking even,' he said carefully. 'I haven't had a chance to look at the books, of course. I can't really say anything until I do that.'

The two men conferred. Was he imagining his growing sense of insinuation in Silva's tone? He began to feel rather sick. The mingled odours of salt, fish, sewage and engine exhaust were in the room, from the adjacent harbour area. Had Frank been approached for a bribe? Licences . . .

'Driscoll was a hard-working, experienced restaurant manager?'

'Yes . . . Why?'

'And you made a large investment in a country you did not know, and you trusted him entirely to manage the investment?'

'I told you. I've known him ten years. He was my friend.'

'The amount of the investment?'

'I don't see . . . fifty thousand dollars.'

Silva spoke to Batista, apparently translating the amount into escudos. The captain rolled his eyes in comic disbelief, and laughed. He spoke, gesturing toward Reade with the green American passport in his hand.

'What's he saying?' Reade asked.

'The property belonged to his wife's cousin,' Silva said. 'He understands now why the cousin talked about stupid rich

Americans. I'm sorry, but you did ask.'

Silva did not look sorry.

Batista spoke again. He was not laughing any more.

'And Senhor Driscoll was a military man?'

'Well . . . no. He tended bar. Sometimes he got acting jobs . . .'

'And he had no military experience? You are sure? Vietnam? Middle East? He was not in Lebanon in 1958?'

'He was in the Korean war. He got drafted when he finished college and he spent a couple of years in the army. He told war stories . . . But that doesn't make him a military man. You asked if he was . . .'

Both men leaned forward intently.

'In Korea? He was captured by the Communists?'

Reade laughed shortly. 'Of course not. He spent all his time in Japan.'

'Did he use drugs?'

'No, no. He drank . . .'

'Do you use drugs?'

'No. What *is* all this? I just made a business investment, that's all.'

'My questions are quite serious, Mr Reade.'

'So are my answers.'

'What are your political sympathies?'

Politics, for the second time that interminable day. Black Panthers, Weathermen, Richard Nixon. 'I left America

53

to get away from politics,' Reade said. Batista was leafing slowly through Reade's passport, looking up from each page to stare at him as if he could read illicit ports of entry in his face. In the waning light the policeman's head seemed to have been carved out of black stone.

'And Mr Driscoll. I assume he had no politics either?'

'Oh, for Christ's sake, Frank was even less political than I am. Can't you see . . . we came here to get away from all that . . . to forget problems . . .'

Silva took a blue pack of Gauloises from his pocket, and offered it to Reade, who refused. He took one himself and lighted it with a pocket lighter.

'You are a stranger in Portugal,' he said, reflectively blowing out smoke. 'I must tell you that these are trying times for us. We are a poor country, beset on all sides. We are fighting the Communists in Angola. The country is filled with refugees from Africa. There is always talk of discontent, of revolution.'

'I thought the government had everything under its thumb,' Reade said nastily.

Silva smiled. He reported the remark to Batista, who grunted.

'We hope to keep it that way,' Silva said. 'You must understand that we have to watch enterprises like yours in these parlous times.

A large amount of foreign money—and that is a large amount by our standards, we are a poor people—invested by people without real business credentials. The kind of establishment that could become a gathering place for all sorts of elements—we have been told that the Casabranca catered to resident aliens and members of our armed forces, officers and other ranks. Young people, often restless and discontented.' He flicked ash on the floor. 'Then the *patrão* dies mysteriously. We must be aware . . .'

'But of what?'

'Well . . . Two possibilities. Subversive political activity and smuggling.'

Reade shook his head wearily, despite the feeling of nervousness that assailed him. 'You're out of your mind,' he said.

Silva's expression remained unchanged. 'You continue to maintain then, that you and Driscoll opened this business as two naïve romantics with no knowledge of political and criminal realities? And that your business was not yet profitable? And Driscoll had no private income?'

'Yes, that's right. I maintain that . . .'

'His salary was?'

'About fifty dollars a week, American. Plus room and board, of course, and drinks.' His eyes met Silva's and he felt suddenly guilty. 'That's a good income here,' he said defensively.

Batista thrust papers across the desk. Silva picked them up and handed them to Reade. 'Perhaps you can explain these?' he said politely.

A soggy pile of British currency wrapped in a piece of paper. It was a bearer's note drawn on a Madrid bank for two hundred thousand pesetas.

Reade looked from the notes to Silva, who extinguished his cigarette in an ashtray on the desk. 'They were found,' Silva said, 'in your partner's pockets by the fisherman who pulled him out of the sea.'

Reade heard the words as dull blows on his consciousness.

'I don't know anything about this,' he said. 'I don't even know how much money this is.'

'Over three thousand dollars U.S.'

Reade shook his head. Suddenly Batista slammed his fist on his desk, snapped something at Silva, got up and strode angrily from the room.

Silva shrugged resignedly.

'Since you appear to have nothing more to say, you are free to go. Unfortunately Captain Batista is forced to retain your passport. For the time being. Your restaurant also must remain closed, until this unpleasantness has been cleared up.' He pulled another Gauloise from his pack and lighted it. 'It is well to close it,' he said. 'In Portugal it is traditional, to show respect for the dead.'

56

Reade thought suddenly of the funeral procession at the bridge, and Big Tony's remark, 'Lots of deads.' Now he too had become a mourner. Silva was grinning at him: he felt like a mouse being toyed with by a Cheshire cat.

'The captain will contact you soon,' Silva said. 'Do not leave Giz. Tend to your own business.'

CHAPTER EIGHT

It was a twenty minute drive from Lagos back to the Casabranca. The bar was still locked; Reade could only glimpse the interior through windows obscured by the reflection of the sinking sun. The flat which was set aside for him on the second floor was locked too, but on the top floor the door to Frank's studio apartment stood ajar. The bed-sitting room was a shambles. That was no surprise, really, to anyone who knew Frank, but it crossed Reade's mind that the place had been ransacked. He rejected the idea when he noticed unopened parcels of laundry and boxes of books on the floor among the rumpled clothing, dirty glasses and full ashtrays.

The room was filled with light from french doors which led to a small balcony overlooking the beach. Reade thrust his head out for a moment: the sun was beginning to settle on the orange roofs of the villas which beetled over the cliffs to the west of the village. He left the doors open to the breeze and mentally rolled up his sleeves: physical activity was the only antidote he saw at that moment from the melancholy which he felt; he had lost his friend and his passport. He was vulnerable, bereft, cast adrift on the very property which that morning had given him a comfortable feeling of ownership and of belonging.

The unmade bed stood near the french doors: he pulled off the bedclothes and turned over the mattress. Then he spilled out the contents of the bureau, one drawer at a time. The top drawer held tie-clasps, cuff-links, a whisk broom. The second and third were stuffed with unfolded underwear, trousers and socks. In the bottom drawer were some papers and snapshots. There was one of Frank and the young American, Philip Vandermint, both smiling and wearing Boston Red Sox baseball caps. There was a rather blurred picture of a blonde woman in a one-piece bathing suit. On the back, in large, looping script, were the words, 'Paris, soon. George.' The rest of the stuff—more pictures, postcards, letters, receipts —apparently had been brought from New York.

In the small kitchen alcove, the stove

looked unused. There was a half-empty vodka bottle and a smeared glass in the sink. He opened the refrigerator: a desiccated half-lemon, a straw-covered *garrafão* of red wine, bottles of Worcestershire and Tabasco sauce, a crumpled package of chocolate . . .

He went into the bathroom and fingered his way gingerly through rusty razor blades, shapeless toothpaste tubes . . . there was nothing much in the medicine cabinet.

He sat on the floor in the sitting-room and began to go through the boxes, most of which contained books that he himself had helped Frank to pack in New York. Early editions of the *Village Voice*, City Lights poets—books which Frank had probably never read. Under the bed were a pile of well-thumbed westerns, and crumpled copies of the *International Herald Tribune*. Here was also the box he had been looking for, the one in which Frank stored his personal records.

Characteristically Frank had put everything into large manila envelopes and filed them in the nearest convenient receptacle. One envelope contained the contracts and other documents for the purchase of the Casabranca. Another held personal correspondence from the States, most of it from Reade. A third seemed to be filled with receipts and notices of bills paid. The fourth envelope bulged with unpaid bills, tax forms and dunning notices. For three months, since

March, Frank had apparently not paid any bills for the Casabranca. In March he had settled an unusually large tax assessment. He had not written to Reade about that payment, although their agreement had been that Frank would ask permission to pay any unanticipated sums. Apparently the tax had drained off three months of the operating budget, which was supposed to carry the restaurant until June when both Reade and the tourist season would arrive. June was supposed to see an influx of cash and the first return on their investment.

Reade sat back, absently staring at a final notice from a Portimão butcher named Castro demanding two thousand escudos. Although he could not read the tax assessment notice, it was clear to him that Frank had piled up a deficit of about five thousand American dollars.

Slowly he shoved the papers together and put them back in the box. A paper slipped out. It was a duplicate of the waterlogged bank certificate Batista had shown him; a Spanish bearer's note from the Banco Hispano Americano in Madrid, worth half as much as the other certificate: one hundred thousand pesetas. But that meant that Driscoll had in his possession enough money to cover the Casabranca's bills. But he hadn't paid them.

And now he was dead.

Reade picked up another paper at random. A note from a travel agent in Faro confirming a round trip flight to London for Sr Francis X. Driscoll. Arriving London June 13; departing June 14, with a stopover in Lisbon on the afternoon of June 14. He folded the papers and shoved them in his pocket. Then he took them out again and put them in his billfold, where he had carried his passport.

He had had enough—more than enough—for one day. He was going out for a swim, in the cool sea. He felt hot, sticky and tired.

The beach was deserted. Reade stepped into the shallow surf: it ran in foamy fingers over pebbles and sand crabs. He felt the cold at first, then the air seemed colder than the water. He was buffeted upright by a wave, dived into the next wave and breast-stroked under water until he was in over his head. Then he rolled over and floated in the swell. He felt much better; he began to relax. His feet rose and his head sank a little under the rolling sea. He shook his head like a dog, clearing his ears. His mind floated, almost lazily, over the problems he had so suddenly encountered.

Probably he, Michael Reade, who so prided himself on his forethought and organization— and after all, that was what had made him a top model in New York—probably he had made a terrible mistake in sending Frank to

Portugal on his own. Had he been irresponsible? Were those things he knew about, those things he had shrugged off—Frank's loose way with the truth, his personal messiness, his drinking, which when you looked at it squarely was really not just social drinking—weren't those the things he should have thought of before he walked into this arrangement . . . ?

Chill invaded his bones. He began to swim back to the beach. Frank had arrived in December with a six-month plan and the money to put it into effect. And he *had* put it into effect, really: the building had been renovated, staff had been hired, supplies had been purchased, and a small but steady clientele had been developed: year-round foreign residents, and week-ending *Lisbonenses*. Then in March the government had entered the picture: for some reason the amount of tax required was quadruple what had been expected, and Frank had paid it. Consequently all the cash he had came from daily receipts, which had to be small during the rainy winter and cold early spring. So Frank couldn't pay his bills.

He had decided to moonlight, to keep afloat somehow until fresh reserves came in. How? Something illegal? Did the police know Frank was short of cash? But why hadn't he told Reade . . . why hadn't he asked for more money? The tax assessment wasn't his fault.

Reade came out of the sea near the ramp where Frank had been dumped that morning, and walked up the boat landing, wincing at the feel of the rough stone under his feet.

Why, indeed? Reade knew that Frank was a melodramatic, undisciplined drinker. But he was also a dedicated hard worker. And Reade had ignored the first set of qualities and concentrated on the second. He had dismissed Frank's obvious problems as charming eccentricities. Frank was so loyal. But that was it, wasn't it? A drunken, fanatically loyal, insecure person, theatrical . . . He would do anything rather than let Reade down.

He looked up at the french windows of Frank's apartment. Something seemed to move there. But that was impossible. This whole thing was getting on his nerves. He needed a bath, and some supper and some sleep. Then he would get to the bottom of all this, and he would straighten it all out. He would bring the Casabranca back on course. He jogged the rest of the way across the sand.

In Frank's bathroom, which could certainly have used a scrubbing-up, he pulled off his bathing trunks, and tossed them into the sink. He slipped into the tub, let the water run, and began to wash the salt water and sand away. When he finished, he took a folded bath towel off a shelf and began to rub himself vigorously. The roughness of the towel, and the cool air from the balcony was stimulating. He flexed his arm muscles and tightened, experimentally, the flat plane of his stomach. Suddenly he felt the stirring of sexual desire, a confirmation of his sense of renewal. He drew some deep breaths, and bent over to touch his toes.

He straightened up when he felt cold steel on his buttocks. His erection died. He felt a chill in his groin.

'Don't turn around, please. Just don't move at all.'

The voice was female.

He dropped the towel and raised his hands in the air.

'Good,' said the woman. '*Sta bom.* Please identify yourself. What is your name? *Como se chama?*'

'I'm Michael Reade. I own this place.'

'Nice try. Reade's not due for two days. Come on. What are you doing here?' The knife pressed painfully into his flesh.

Involuntarily, Reade rose to his tiptoes. 'I'm telling the truth. I got here early. Look in my pants pocket. There's an international drivers licence.'

After a moment the pressure of the knife eased, and, out of the corner of his eye, he saw her stoop and pick up his trousers from the floor with one hand while she pointed the knife at him with the other. She was the woman in Frank's snapshot. She was deeply tanned and her short hair was sun-streaked; she was wearing a low-necked print blouse and white slacks.

She found the licence and looked at the photograph on it, then back at Reade with enormous violet eyes. She looked down at the picture again. There were wrinkles around her eyes, which were red. She had been crying. She was a beautiful woman who would never see thirty again.

She looked sadly at Reade and dropped the licence and the serrated kitchen knife onto his trousers on the floor. Then she walked slowly to the bed and sat on the bare mattress.

'Another country heard from,' she said bitterly. 'I suppose you've heard.'

'I was at the bar next door when they brought the body in.'

'Poor bugger.' It was unclear whether she was referring to Frank or to Reade. 'Well,' she said, 'Frank did say you were good-looking. You've been sunbathing all day?'

Feeling foolish, Reade picked up the towel and wrapped it around his hips. 'No, of course not,' he said. 'The police. In Lagos.'

'Bastards. Do they know anything?'

'He was last seen in Sagres, last night. At a bar.'

'*Tubarão*. The Shark Bar. How did he ever . . . ?' She stood up suddenly and gestured to the boxes on the floor. 'I suppose you're the one who went through Frank's things?'

Reade nodded.

'So you know about the financial situation.'

'Somewhat.'

'Somewhat,' she echoed, mockingly. 'It's a bloody mess, isn't it? Frank said you were always cautious. Now are you ready to go to Sagres and do something about all this?'

'What could we find in Sagres that the police haven't . . .'

'Oh, don't ask so many questions. Are you going to do something about this, I said, or are you going to sit back meekly and let them confiscate your business? And send you packing back to the States with your tail between your legs?'

'I'm willing,' Reade said defensively. 'I'm cautious, yes—that doesn't mean I'm afraid, you know.'

She smiled, a genuine smile. 'I haven't said you're afraid. Frank said you had guts. In your own way. All right, good, let's go then. We can talk in the car. And bring your toothbrush. You can stay with me.' She silenced his protest with a wave of the hand. 'Your flat here isn't furnished; I don't suppose you want to doss down in Frank's leavings.'

He picked up his clothing, hanging precariously to the towel, and headed for the bathroom.

'Oh,' she said, 'I'm Georgia Ryan.'

66

'So I guessed,' he said drily.

'By the way . . .'

'Yes?'

Reade was about to close the bathroom door.

She looked amused, and suddenly much younger.

'What were you thinking about when you were touching your toes?'

Reade slammed the door.

CHAPTER NINE

Georgia Ryan gripped the wheel of her Ford Cortina; the nails of her ringless hands were painted blood red. 'I've been wondering how to begin,' she said. 'You're the golden boy, reeking with success and money. Maybe you wouldn't understand.'

The landscape west of Giz was desolate. Dusty hills blocked the view of the sea; the farms were mean affairs with houses like chicken coops. A harnessed donkey dragged itself around a decrepit water mill; smoke came from an ancient brick kiln; dung was everywhere—it certainly accounted for a good deal of the 'smell of Africa'. Big Tony had taken up more than Frank's physical mannerisms.

'The whole thing is simple,' Georgia said.

'Frank and I were both short of funds. He had tax problems; I had other kinds of problems. I didn't have anyone to turn to; Frank had you, but he refused to turn to you . . . Anyway, I knew some people in Albufeira . . . Englishmen . . . who knew a Portuguese who wanted to dispose of some cash. They wanted to invest in a bar or restaurant . . . get the money back as legitimate earnings . . . Frank and I were to be paid a percentage . . . I mean, I was the one who put them in touch with Frank . . .'

She twitched the radio on, and then twitched it off again.

'So on Tuesday afternoon I drove Frank to Portimão to catch the airport taxi. He was flying to Lisbon to meet someone who had the money, pick it up and bring it back here on Wednesday to deposit it in the bank . . . gradually . . . as profits. I drove to Faro Wednesday to meet him, but he wasn't on the plane. So I met the next plane, and then the one after that—the last one. I didn't know what the hell happened . . . I stayed there for the night, in a hotel . . . It was bloody awful.

'The next morning there were two planes . . . then I thought he might be trying to reach me in Giz. I walked into the bar of the club, and Clive Mowbray told me . . .' Her voice shook. 'I thought they killed him for the money . . . I went to the Casabranca, I didn't know what else to do. I heard you

68

coming up the stairs. I thought you were one of them. Well, you can't blame me, can you?'

She was not telling the truth, but the question was, did she know she was lying? Actually, he might know more of the truth than she did. Reade felt an upsurge of painful anger at Frank who had made such a mess of everything.

'How can you be sure he was murdered?' he said. 'The police didn't say he was.'

'The police,' she said. 'Who? Batista?'

'Yes, and an interpreter named Silva.'

'Interpreter! Silva is head of PIDE for this region. Batista takes his orders from him.'

He could not say he was surprised; he had suspected that.

'Well, anyway, you don't know Frank was murdered. Why are we rushing off like this to Sagres?'

'I want to look for Frank's bag. I think he might have left it at the Shark Bar . . .'

'And the Portuguese investors?'

'I talked to the English go-betweens. They don't know anything, but they want me to try and find that bag. It had the money in it, it was given to him. It's incriminating, they're anxious to retrieve it.'

'Who are these people?'

She looked straight ahead.

'Maybe it's better for you not to know,' she said. 'Frank knew. And look what happened to him.'

'So you suspect them?'

She pulled into a bus stop and slammed on the brakes. A cluster of peasant women with folded parasols looked at them curiously.

'Listen,' she said tensely. 'I don't know what happened to Frank. I spent two bloody days hanging around waiting for him, and I'm sick of hanging around. The Portuguese are good at it, but I'm not. I suppose you're good at it too. Frank said you were fucking cautious—'

'You listen!' Reade shouted. 'There's no point in getting pissed off at me. How do you think I feel about this? But you're not interested in anyone else's feelings. Frank—was my friend longer than he was yours—'

'Oh God,' she said. She buried her hands in her face and began to cry. 'I don't want to be nasty to you,' she said in a muffled voice. 'I need you. I trust you—'

Touched, he put his arm around her shoulders. He needed someone too. But did he trust her?

She lowered her hands, and smiled at him, then wiped her face with the back of her hand, and put the car back in gear. 'Fancy this,' she said. 'This isn't the way Frank wanted us to get together. Poor Frank. He wanted to fix us up, did he tell you?'

'But I thought you and he . . .'

'We tried it once. But it didn't work, you

70

know. Frank was a boozer. I'm afraid I like a sober lover . . .'

She touched the back of his hand. Reade felt his scepticism slip somewhat. He should know better, he thought . . .

'Here's Sagres,' she said.

Sagres was an unremarkable village; its two headlands jutted into the ocean on the south, and Cape St. Vincent to the east. The Bar Tubarão was housed in a grey stone building with a wooden sign; a crude shark's head was painted on it.

'You'd better stay in the car,' Georgia said. 'I know the owner. He's a suspicious bugger. He'll open up more freely if I talk to him alone.'

Her perfume lingered in the car after her. Reade stretched his legs and yawned.

Then she was at the car window.

'Let's walk,' she said.

Reade scrambled out of the car, and they began to walk toward the sea.

'The bag's not there,' she said. 'Frank got here last night at eight, on the bus from Lisbon. He stayed in the bar until ten and then he left. He had the bag with him. One of the fishermen saw him heading out here toward the *furnas*.'

'*Furnas?*' Reade said. 'Is that anything like a stove? Somebody at the club this morning said something about a cold stove league.'

She looked at him. 'Who've you been

71

talking to at the club?'

'Guy named Vandermint? An American. D'you know him? And a woman named Lucy, and Clive Mowbray?'

'They're a bad lot,' Georgia said. 'Too much money, too much booze. They didn't do Frank any good, I'll tell you that. I think he admired them, if you want the truth.'

'But what's the cold stove league?'

She shrugged. 'Never heard of it. I suppose Vandermint read about it in one of his stupid magazines. More money than brains.'

'Well, what's the *furnas*?'

'You'll see.'

A kind of bright dusk had fallen, and the air had grown perceptibly cooler. A mist began to creep in from the water. To the left, or the east, the Howard Johnson orange of the modern government *pousada* on the headland gradually disappeared into the fog. They took a westerly path to the Sagres peninsula: the effect was like walking onto a runway carved out of ebony. He heard the moan of the sea; the pathway verged the edge of the sheer cliff.

'Why in hell would Frank come out here in the middle of the night?' he asked nervously. 'It's pretty spooky here.'

'Looks like bloody Dartmoor with this fog,' she said.

The sky had disappeared. Everything was black. Suddenly a face appeared, floating on air. Reade gasped. They stood staring; there was the sound of the crash of the waves at the foot of the cliffs and a far-off sound of thunder.

Georgia spoke in Portuguese and the face answered. It was only a peasant with a long pole who had been fishing from the cliffs. His boots squeaked as he moved off down the path.

'I asked him about Frank,' Georgia said. 'He didn't see him himself, but last night his nephew saw a tall *Anglo* carrying a bag; he says he went down the last pathway near the big *furna* just after dark.'

She plunged ahead in the mist, her white trousers giving off a spectral gleam. Reade followed her hastily.

The haze lifted momentarily; he saw they were passing a huge fortress.

'Prince Henry the Navigator,' Georgia said. 'His former digs.' She seemed very excited.

She stopped suddenly. They were at the edge of the cliffs. Reade could just make out the foaming turbulence of the sea far below, battering whitely against the rocks. A menacing crescendo emanated from the darkness. First there was a dull rumble and slap of the sea where the surf broke; this was drowned in a rhythmic sequence of dull explosions. They sounded like detonations deep in the earth, like the rumble of thunder. Then there was a deep sigh, which seemed to

73

shake the vegetation of the headland.

'What is *that*?' Reade asked. He was beginning to think he had been very foolish to follow her unquestioningly up here.

'Don't be afraid,' she said. 'Those are the *furnas*, love. Their bark is worse than their bite. They sound like a giant breathing, don't they? Look!'

She pointed to a giant fissure in the rock which lay before the tip of the peninsula. Reade could make out dark spots on the face of the cliffs below them. They were caves: flecks of foam spat around them. Like foam around the mouths of mad dogs, he thought, dramatically. The thunderclap sounded, then a long sigh from the fissure in the rock, and then the eruption of foamy white water from the caves.

'That cleft in the rock goes all the way down below sea level,' Georgia shouted above the racket. 'It forms a system of fissures with the caves in the cliff face. The booming comes from the sea driving into the caves . . . It thunders when the boom carries up through the fissure. Then the water spews into the sea . . . You hear that sigh . . .'

'And Frank came here?' he shouted back. 'Why?'

'. . . don't . . . meet . . .'

Her words were erased by the explosion from the *furna*. Would Frank meet someone in this desolate, dangerous place? Was he supposed to hand the money over here? Did he . . . did he *fall* here? An accident . . .

A perfect place for an accident.

'Let's go back,' he called, touching her shoulder.

She shook her head, and walked precariously down the path which wound down the face of the cliff. He paused a moment and then began to follow her, reluctantly. He didn't want to look like a coward in front of a woman. But . . .

The spray blew in his face.

'A wild goose chase!' he said, when he caught up to her.

She stopped. 'The caves start here,' she said. 'There are a few we can enter, that are safe, they're above the surf line.' She turned her head toward him; her hair was wet. 'Maybe he hid the bag in one of them. Let's look.'

He hesitated. 'It'll only take a minute,' she said, and plunged ahead into the cave.

The surf line seemed very close to him. Reluctantly he followed her again, touching the clammy cave walls with exploratory fingers. The smell of fish and salt was strong. She stopped suddenly, and he bumped against her.

'This is crazy,' he said. 'I can't see a thing.'

'I should have brought a torch,' she said.

The crash of the sea against the rocks sounded very close.

'It's hopeless,' she said. He was close enough to feel her hair lightly touching his face. Then suddenly the noise was overwhelming. His mouth was full of salt; he smelled rot everywhere. There was an evil eye hanging over him. As he turned toward the mouth of the cave he heard a mighty roar, the crash of thunder, and a long sigh.

Then he was falling.

CHAPTER TEN

He came to, awash in salt water, wedged against a pile of large stones an arm's length from the mouth of the cave. He rose shakily to his feet. The sky had cleared; the young moon was rising over the cape. He could see the star-like twinkle of a cluster of fishing boats at the base of the cliffs.

He had very nearly followed Frank to the grave. He felt as though he had swallowed salt water. He had been unconscious . . . why was he still alive? Where were his attackers now? Where was Georgia? She had been in front of him when he turned toward the cave mouth.

In the moonlight he could see the surf breaking against the cliff a half mile to the south. The undulating white ribbon of the breaker worked its way from south to north, curling and crashing, curling and crashing, attacking the line of lower caves. The water, forced up by the tides below, spewed out of the caves at the level where he stood.

Suddenly he thought he saw what had happened. When they entered the cave the surf was about to pound into the cave directly below them. When it did that, the turbulent water was driven up the fissure into their cave where it exploded . . . Its force carried him bodily back out onto the path. The stone enclosure had saved him from being washed over the cliff entirely.

And where was Georgia? A dribble of water was running out of the cave . . .

The sea was turning to foam, clenching and breaking closer and closer to where he was standing . . . Wet and stiff, he plunged into the cave in his clumsy clothes with his shoes squishing. He felt a joyous leap of the heart: she was on her knees on the cave floor, moving . . .

'You're all right,' he said.

She turned her head and smiled at him wanly.

'Had my wind knocked out,' she said.

'We've got to get out of here,' he said. 'There'll be more water soon.'

He helped her up; the detonations were edging closer. It was not easy to move; she leaned on him rather heavily, and the water in his shoes did not help. The surf crashed up into the next cave as it withdrew, he heard the now familiar sounds.

He pushed Georgia down, behind a block-like formation of stone on the floor of the cave and crouched over her. The stone was a natural barrier reef . . . The cave exploded, the powerful agitated water washed over them. He held his breath . . .

Then it was over. He felt a sense of exhilaration: he had proven himself in a kind of trial by water. He scrambled up, and Georgia followed him, gasping for breath. Together they climbed up the path until they were out of reach of the sea.

★   ★   ★

'You saved my life,' she said. The *patrão* of the *Tubarão* had provided them with towels and blankets. They sat huddled together in a corner before a small space heater, sipping the clear, fiery *medronho*.

'What did you expect me to do? Walk off and leave you in the cave? To tell the truth, I never expected to see you there . . .'

Their eyes met.

'To tell the truth,' he said, 'I thought you pushed me.'

Her mouth twisted wryly, and she continued to look him in the eye. They were distracted by a considerable racket at the door. Some outlandish guests had arrived. An enormous figure in a white burnous lumbered over to them.

'What a coincidence,' it said, in an English accent. 'We've been looking for you.'

The white hood slipped back and Reade recognized Clive Mowbray.

'We're mourning Frank in the manner we thought he'd enjoy,' Mowbray said. 'An Irish wake, with theatrical trimmings. Whatever are you doing?'

'We dropped in for a swim,' Georgia said.

Lucy Luce came up, in a jewelled cape; Vandermint was with her, wearing some kind of khaki combat gear.

'It was too deadly,' Lucy said. 'No Casabranca, and the English bar in Lagos was really a bore, full of Germans . . . But what are you supposed to be? All these towels. Anyway, I'm glad you found each other.'

Her speech was somewhat slurred, and her eyes glittered.

'Do come join us,' Mowbray said. 'It won't seem like a wake without you.'

He smiled jovially, and went back to join his party: Vandermint and a slender woman in a man's smoking jacket. Lucy slid into a chair next to them.

'Lovely and warm here,' she said, 'isn't it? I think Philip looks absolutely smashing, don't you? He bought that uniform from a drunken soldier at the Abrigo, you know, absolutely eons ago, and now it came in so handy, for Frank's sake.'

'Have some *medronho*,' Reade said. He signalled the landlord.

'You really are thoughtful,' Lucy said. 'I can't help admiring your thoughtfulness. Have you got a match?'

'We really ought to be going,' Georgia said.

'Why, your hair is soaking wet, dear,' Lucy said. 'You can't go out with wet hair. You'll catch your death. Have you been swimming?'

'No,' Georgia said. 'I just worked up a heavy sweat.'

'Well, that really is terribly funny,' Lucy said vaguely. 'You look as though you've been swimming. But I must have been misinformed.'

She closed one large mascaraed eye at Reade.

'Get it?' she said. '"I must have been misinformed." Frank said that, you remember.'

Georgia looked at Reade.

'It's from *Casablanca*,' he said, apologetically. For some reason he felt embarrassed. 'The movie, you know. The French cop asks Bogart why he came to Casablanca, and Bogart says he came for the waters. And the cop looks—Claude Raines, you know. He looks surprised, and he says there are no waters in Casablanca. It's in the desert. And Bogart says, "I was misinformed".'

Lucy Luce's laughter filled the room. 'Yes, that's it,' she said. '"I was misinformed." Really, Frank was a riot.'

'This is really a barrel of laughs,' Georgia said, 'but I'm afraid we have to be going.'

'Oh, must you? But the party hasn't started yet.'

'I've had a rather long day,' Reade said. He began to slide out of the cocoon of blankets.

'I'd like a word with you.' It was Mowbray back again. 'Can you spare me a moment?'

'Sure,' Reade said. He rose, feeling quite stiff, and walked a short distance away with the Englishman. He glanced back at Georgia: her wet hair was plastered in spikes across her forehead; her large lavender eyes signalled distress at being left with Lucy. He held up his hand in a placatory way to her.

Mowbray's face looked flushed against the white robe he was wearing; his insignificant nose was streaked with tiny red veins.

'I merely wanted to express my condolences to you,' he said, in a low voice, 'and—to offer you assistance if you need it. I was awfully fond of Frank . . .' His blue eyes were watery.

'That's awfully kind of you,' Reade said, touched.

'Frank came to me, you know,' Mowbray said, 'when he was having trouble with the taxes. I was able to help him a little, I think. It was only a pittance . . .'

Apparently everyone in the world but Reade had known about Frank's problems. 'Of course I'll pay you back,' he said stiffly. 'Just give me the amount. And interest . . .'

'Now, now,' Mowbray said. 'Don't get your back up. I had every intention of being paid back; I never thought for a moment that I wouldn't. I only brought it up now to let you know that I have a personal interest—besides boozing, of course—in your charming establishment. I want to offer some continuing support until things ease up. After all,' he added seriously, 'the loss of a man like Frank . . .'

Reade felt foolish. He was behaving like an oaf. Georgia's rather unbending hostility had rubbed off on him, perhaps, or he took a more proprietary interest in Frank than really made sense.

'I'm really awfully sorry, Clive,' he said. 'It's been a damned long day and my nerves are on edge. I'm sure you understand. I appreciate what you did—and your offer . . . I need to look at the books, you understand . . .'

'Well, we'll talk about it when you get yourself settled,' Mowbray said heartily. Georgia had extricated herself from Lucy and came up to them.

'Can we go?' she said flatly.

'You do look wet,' Mowbray said. 'Really night bathing?'

'How much was it?' Reade said. 'It's on the books, I take it?'

. 'Now, I can't even remember,' Mowbray said. 'This isn't the time. With Frank . . . I only wanted to . . .'

★   ★   ★

'I can't stand those people,' she said, when they were in the car.

'No, I could see that,' Reade said. 'Who are they, really?'

'The idle rich. Can't you tell?'

'Well, I mean . . . I suppose Lucy's a rich widow? And I know about Vandermint. What about Mowbray?'

'He's married to money,' Georgia said. 'Mines in Canada.'

'Where is she?'

'Oh, she stays home, I hear. At their house in the hills. It sounds Victorian. Rochester's wife locked up . . . But she puts in an appearance occasionally at the club. One of those mousy washed-out English women, you know, print dresses and pearls. He worked once. In Singapore, and then I heard they had a ranch in . . . oh, one of those colonial places. They're awfully boring, the whole lot of them. What was he telling you?'

'Oh, nothing much. Something about a bill.'

* * *

Helmut Zeigler gritted his teeth. Turner Cromwell, the trouble-shooter from World Communications, was swirling the 1918 Armagnac in his glass and discoursing, at length, on the fact that it had been placed in barrels at the time of the armistice after World War I and then had lain, serenely, in that same oak until four years after the Nazis were sent home. Zeigler had come to talk business, not about brandy. He, and the other bankers, knew what had happened now on the transmission from London to Madrid, knew too well. What they were looking for from Cromwell was a display of the intuition, and willingness to put that intuition into action, for which the man was well-known. Instead, he had now had to sit for two hours and watch the transplanted American consume course after course of the special menu he had arranged with the chef—at the expense, of course, of the Vorot: a mousse of *Omble Chevalier*, just caught in *Lac Annecy*, which the restaurant overlooked; *queues d'ecrevisse*, imported, Cromwell sadly confided, from Yugoslavia; saddle of local lamb, very rare; Belgian endive in hazelnut oil from the Perigord; and so on, into the *sorbet* and pastries. The crowning blow had been the bottle of 1953 Château Petrus, at 200 francs, which had been found in the cellar at

84

Cromwell's urging.

Zeigler picked at his food and drank Perrier; he had a duodenal ulcer. He had been warned of Cromwell's extravagant *gourmandise*, but his patience was wearing thin.

Finally, after ostentatiously inspecting his watch, he caught Cromwell's eye.

'Ah,' said the American, peering over the edge of the balloon glass, 'you want to know what I think about our little theft, I expect.'

'Indeed.'

'First of all, you have to be looking two ways: to Switzerland, and to Iberia.'

'Yes,' said Zeigler, leaning forward, his dark suit stark against the immaculate white tablecloth. He had hoped for something more original than this line of thought.

Cromwell had picked up the look in his eye: 'Of course you're aware that the man who conceived this operation is intimate with foreign exchange markets, Swiss banks, and is probably indeed an insider, probably,' he raised his eyebrows ironically, 'even Swiss.'

'Not necessarily,' Zeigler responded, unintentionally defensive: a knee-jerk response.

Cromwell burped discreetly into his napkin. There was a twinkle in his eyes: 'Well, no one knows better than a Swiss that his own countrymen, the bankers at any rate, would allow their grandmothers to be sodomized by a pack of oil sheikhs before acknowledging to the authorities that they had been duped, or taking a chance on having to open their books.'

Zeigler decided to ignore the insolence this time. He sipped some Perrier, and called to the waiter for the check.

'But of course,' Cromwell went on, 'our Swiss is the last man we look for.'

Zeigler was momentarily startled: 'And why is that?'

'Because he knows what he's doing. Too well, probably, to be ferreted out without one hell of a lot of misery. Particularly for us.'

'So?' Zeigler presented his credit card to the waiter.

'So we go after the weak links. This character in London, the sun-tanned bibulous one. He's unreliable. If, of course, they've been stupid enough to allow him to live.'

'They?'

'We have to assume there's some kind of control running the operation in Spain as well as in Switzerland. They sent the money to Spain and Greece, two Mediterranean countries with right-wing governments. This suggests to me that the Iberian end is hooked up in some way to the sort of neo-Nazi illicit cash channels that flourish there, particularly in Madrid. There was something called The Emergency Colonial Relief Fund that was running billions, mostly from West Germany,

86

through Switzerland, to Spain. Then I suppose it ended up in South America or Africa, suppressing left-wing revolutions.'

He stared into the Armagnac for a while, then drank it off in a gulp. 'But mostly I'm thinking of Portugal.'

Zeigler looked up from signing the check. He made sure the waiter had maintained his discreet distance.

'Portugal?'

'It's as right-wing as Greece or Spain, but has a history of so-called neutrality, and as a place where gold moves surreptitiously. Right next to Spain. If one were to keep it in Spain—the money, that is—they would be taking a big chance on being muscled in on by the neo-Nazis and their friends. A smart thief would move it out of Spain right quick. And the cardinal rule of money-washing is that you have it simon-pure before you bring it home. Home is where the weak links are—the guy who made all the noise in London and the people down south who took him on as an associate. Probably in Portugal.'

'So you'll go there first?' Zeigler was at once dubious and impressed. The process which Cromwell suggested was the reverse of what he expected and, besides, the primary goal of the Vorot was to find, and *deal with quietly*, the Swiss, as Cromwell called him. Still, it made sense. And moving the scene south provided more room to move around in, without upsetting the authorities at home. And the trail should still lead inevitably back to the source of the swindle.

Cromwell was shrugging his shoulders: 'Eventually Portugal, I assume. But first, one pantleg at a time. First London, then Madrid.' His mouth turned down at the corners in a mock pout. 'Two towns where you have to be a snob to get a good meal. If you can get one at all. I'd much rather be taking a slow boat down the Rhone.'

★   ★   ★

Reade lay naked under the sheets, feeling very cool and clean. Through the windows he could see the flood-lit terraced gardens which ran from the villa to the cliffs overlooking Praia da Giz.

There was a rapid tap on the door and Georgia came in and sat on the edge of the large bed. She was wearing a pale blue bathrobe and she smelled of soap. Her scrubbed face glowed.

'I hope I'm not disturbing you,' she said. 'I hope I didn't tear you away from the wake. Did you know that Irish wakes were originally sexy affairs? Grotesque, but sexy. That little group may be grotesque, but if there's anything they're not, it's sexy. The early wakes were committed to regeneration, you know.'

'I didn't know,' Reade said lazily. Banter was in the air. 'How did you get to be such an expert on wakes?'

'I'm educated,' she said. 'I studied archaeology in Dublin. We learned all about ancient wakes . . .'

The robe fell open a few inches.

'Did you know that people at those wakes took off their clothes . . . sometimes the women would dress in men's clothes . . . and then a candle or a bottle would be placed upright between the legs of the poor dead man, and the mourners would dance around the coffin.'

The skin of her breasts was white against the brown of her chest.

'Our lecturer put it very well: "Games culminating in sexual congress would then ensue." Isn't that well put? His name was Shields. The lecturer. Listen,' she said, standing up, and pulling the sash on her robe tight, 'I'll show you an ancient wake ritual. You're the only available male, so you'll have to pretend you're the corpse.'

'A little morbid,' he said.

'Oh, I don't think you'll be depressed by it. Now.' She moved to the foot of the bed and stood there with her arms raised. 'Lie flat and close your eyes. Pull the sheet up to your chin. Right.'

Reade lay still. His toe twitched self-consciously; her fingers pinched it into immobility. He felt pleasantly drowsy.

'This first stage is called "The Making of the Ship".'

He heard a rustling and felt a momentary breeze past his face.

'Don't peek,' she said. 'Once you've started, you must follow the rules to the finish. Lie still. You're supposed to be dead. And I, you see, am a young local matron of ancient Hibernia preparing you for a spiritual resurrection through the flesh.'

There was a pause. He did not feel quite so drowsy now. He saw coffins in his mind's eye, naked dancers in a red gloaming, goblins . . . He heard the click of the latch.

'The next step,' she said, 'is "The Laying of the Keel". No rude jokes, please.'

The sheet began to be withdrawn with tantalizing slowness from his body: shoulders, nipples, stomach, genitals, thighs, knees, ankles, feet were gradually exposed. His flesh tingled in the sea air from the open window.

She sighed, and then said, in a low voice near his cheek, 'Don't breathe a word. You've not yet come back to life.'

The bed creaked; she stretched out beside him.

'This,' she whispered breathily, 'is called "Forming Stem and Stern".'

Her knee brushed the side of his leg; he felt a sequence of delicate hair's-breadth palpitations as she adjusted her body to the contours of his.

'Next,' she said, 'comes "Erecting the Mast", I see we shall not require a bottle or a candlestick in this particular instance.'

He opened his mouth.

'Shh,' she said. Her hands were weighing down the pillow on each side of his head, and her knees were creating slopes in the mattress on each side of his body. He opened his eyes. Her face was directly above his; her breath was in his nostrils.

'I can't seem to remember the next step,' she said, lowering herself onto him. 'I'm afraid we'll have to im . . . pro . . . vise . . .'

When they finally rolled apart, he raised himself on one elbow and looked into her large languid eyes. 'And what did the ancient Irish call that?'

'That last part? Oh, that, my darling, is called "Drawing the Ship Out of the Mud". Really. You can look it up. *Studies in Celtic Ritual*, volume thirty-seven . . .'

After a moment she said, 'The Irish really hate sex, you know. I often give thanks to the Blessed Virgin that I am half-English.'

'I'd like to thank her too,' Reade said. 'Will I have to die to do it again?'

'That depends,' she said, 'on your definition of dying. There's an archaic meaning, you know . . .'

Laughing, they rolled together, again.

CHAPTER ELEVEN

At daybreak on Friday the phone rang in the spartan bedroom on the north shore of the Zurichsee. Hans Hauptmann picked it up at once. It was Walter Zwingli.

'*Mein Herr.* Forgive me for calling at such an hour. But I thought you would be interested. Herr Zeigler of Crédit Suisse dined last night with an officer of World Communications in the Haute Savoie. They returned together to Geneva and now they have flown to London in the bank's jet. They are staying at the Dorchester.'

'Ah. They go to visit Lloyds.'

'Unquestionably, *mein Herr.*'

'I shall be at my office at nine, Walter.'

Hauptmann put the phone quietly back on the cradle, and turned over, pulling the coverlet up to his chin. How they would squirm at Lloyds trying to explain it! And Zcigler, in a scnsc on suffcrancc with thc World Communications people . . .

And no police. The thought that the banks were afraid to call in the police was almost a lascivious one. He rolled over onto his stomach, and ground his pelvis into the feather mattress.

Suddenly he stopped. There was one thing. The woman. She and the London trouble-maker had come into the picture together. But no one had mentioned her. He could not be sure that she was now out of the picture as well. And she knew about Cold Stove.

He propped himself on his elbow and turned on the light. Should he send a telex? No. He had sent too many already, perhaps. In the interest of security the fewer sent the better. He did not want the official in Portugal to think he was losing his nerve. He would have to hope that she had been taken care of, or at least that she was more reliable than he in fact knew any woman could be.

CHAPTER TWELVE

The room had tall casement windows and overlooked a pleasant garden. A man in a smock wheeled in a coffee tray.

'I should like you to meet our Mr Anderson,' Lord Annal said, in a deep, resonant voice. 'Mr Cromwell, Mr Zeigler. Do please sit down, Mr Anderson. We are relying on you to illuminate this unfortunate occurrence for us.'

Anderson, looking rather white, and with a bandage on the crown of his head, slipped into his chair at the round mahogany table, roughly across from the two visitors from

Switzerland. Briefly he talked about his encounter with Mr Eliot.

'The machine used for incoming messages from eastern Europe was open,' he said. 'Of course. It was the machine Lambourne had been using when I first entered the office with this man. I checked, despite . . .'

'Mr Anderson insisted on checking personally,' Lord Annal said. 'Even though he was of course badly hurt, and he had been tied up for over an hour.' He sipped coffee from a thin china cup.

'We appreciate that,' Cromwell said.

'The money transfer machine for outgoing messages to the East had been used, too,' Anderson said. 'We checked the transmission slips. Lambourne had of course handled messages during the night, but there was an additional transmission: the directive to the Crédit Suisse, as you are aware. A confirmation code had been requested . . .'

'Do have some coffee, Mr Anderson,' Lord Annal said.

'Thank you, my lord,' Anderson said. 'Not just now. I have to tell you,' he said to Cromwell, 'that this awful thing would never have happened if my Telemometer were in use. I invented it myself, you see, and it was because of that that I encountered this Mr Eliot in the first place.'

'I'm all ears,' Cromwell said.

'I frequently attend conventions in the field

of electronic communications. That is my passion, and also my avocation if I may say so. Last April I attended such a convention in Paris, and met by chance over cocktails a man by the name of Roberto de Vicenzo. He represented himself as an agent for an American who was interested in security problems. One thing led to another, and I mentioned my invention . . . the—'

'The Telemometer,' Cromwell said sympathetically.

'Yes, quite.' Anderson looked at him for a moment. 'When Eliot phoned me last week I had almost forgotten about it . . . He expressed a desire to see the present situation . . . and to discuss the Telemometer. That is a device which transmits the fingerprints of anyone sending a telex message to a computerized element on the receiving end. Authorized fingerprints would of course have been stored in the computer. Fingerprints, as everyone knows, cannot be forged.'

'They always find a way, don't they?' Lord Annal said, to no one in particular.

'We don't have to make it easy for them, my lord,' Anderson said, 'if you don't mind my saying so.'

'You made no attempt to investigate this . . . Mr Eliot . . . before you agreed to meet him?'

'I saw no reason to,' Anderson said. 'I had his card. And I had spoken with him. He was certainly an American. He struck me as a model of an American entrepreneur. A diamond in the rough, if you know what I mean.' He looked at Zeigler, whose face remained impassive.

'And the South American . . .'

'Yes, I've thought about him. He had quite a lot of black hair. It has occurred to me since that he may have been wearing a wig. He was well-dressed. A good suit, and very good shoes. He seemed quite the gentleman.'

Lord Annal smiled nervously.

'Did he speak Spanish?'

'Well, he spoke English quite well. He spoke it as though he had learned it in England. A good accent.'

'But he did not speak in Spanish during the time you were with him?'

'No, why should he?' Mr Anderson said. 'He was Portuguese.'

'Ah,' Zeigler said. 'He told you that?'

'He didn't need to,' Anderson said. 'He rang someone up from the table and spoke in Portuguese. I know it when I hear it, you know; we have had several holidays on the Algarve.'

'Mr Anderson,' Cromwell said softly. 'Do you know that Roberto de Vicenzo is the name of an Argentinian golfer who happens to be the only South American ever to win the British Open?'

'Oh, dear,' Lord Annal said. He smiled.

'One on you, my dear Anderson.'

'I was not aware of that,' Anderson said. 'I'm afraid I have little time to follow sports. Do you think then that this man was an Argentinian?'

'And Thomas S. Eliot . . . of St Louis, wasn't it?'

'What are you going to tell us,' Lord Annal said, cheerily. 'Some sort of film star?'

'Well,' Cromwell said. 'We have reason to believe that both these men gave false names.'

'Well, I should bloody well hope so,' Lord Annal said. 'Damn fools otherwise, eh?'

'From here,' Cromwell announced, 'I shall go to Madrid.'

'Fine, my dear chap,' Lord Annal said. 'We can book you through here if you like. I do wish you luck.'

CHAPTER THIRTEEN

At dawn Reade woke to the eerie sound of crowing cocks, and the braying of a donkey. He shivered in the chill sea breeze, and opened his eyes. Two days ago he had been in New York, listening to ambulance sirens and breathing in car exhaust. Now he was here, and Georgia was with him.

She lay curled away from him. He rose on one elbow, and bent over her. Her lips were parted and a strand of her hair straggled on her cheek. He brushed it away, and pulled the blankets over both of them. She cleared her throat, and burrowed into the pillow.

He fell back again. He was still sleepy. But there were things he had to do . . . to find . . .

He dreamt about wakes. Folding chairs and old women in thick-heeled black shoes and cotton stockings . . . He was standing at the speaker's table at a banquet in a gymnasium. The coffin was in front of the dais; he did not recognize the waxy corpse. The women sat at card tables covered with wrinkled sheets. The scoreboard clock was ticking down. The coach emerged from the locker room door. He was tall, and had red hair. He shouted, 'Feed him, Reade, for Christ's sake! You're responsible! You're the quarter-back! Time is running out!' The old women began to bang knives and forks on the flimsy tables. But there was no ball: what game were they playing? . . . Suddenly he was in the middle of the floor. Vandermint was on one side of him, wearing a combat outfit, and Humphrey Bogart was on the other, in a white linen jacket. Bogart threw a large round ball past Reade to Vandermint, who lofted it back. It was out of Reade's reach. They were playing 'Monkey-in-the-Middle'; that was the game. Reade was the monkey. The crowd was cheering. Not for him. He leaped for the ball but it floated weightlessly away. Desperately, he looked for the coach . . .

Georgia was looking into his face from her pillow. Her feet were intertwined with his.

'Good morning,' she said.

He stared at her. Monkey-in-the-middle, he thought.

Her hands ran down the inside of his thighs.

'Why did you lie to me?' he said.

Her hand stopped. He felt her long fingernails brushing his skin.

'What do you mean?'

'I mean, I want to know why Frank went to London.'

'Lisbon. You mean Lisbon.'

'No. I mean London.'

She turned abruptly away from him, and lay on her back, staring at the ceiling.

'Do you always make love so convincingly to people you think are liars?' she asked bitterly.

'I thought you could explain it,' he said. He was irritated with himself; she had put him on the defensive.

'How did you find out?' she asked, softly.

'I found a travel agent's memo. And he had a lot of money in his pockets when they found him. They turned it over to the police. British money. And a Spanish bearer's note for lots of pesetas. I found another bearer's note in the apartment, also for lots of pesetas.'

She propped herself up on both elbows on the pillow, facing him. Her full breasts dangled toward the bed, pale nipples brushing the patterned sheet.

'I'll tell you the story,' she said. 'But will you help me?'

'Is there some reason why I wouldn't?' he countered. 'But I can't help if I don't know anything.'

She laughed a little. 'You can't help anyway,' she said. 'You haven't got your passport. And the only person who can help me and help you by keeping the Casabranca in business has to have a passport. Because he has to go to Madrid.'

'What about you? You could go yourself.'

'I can't go bloody anywhere. I'm married to a Portuguese you see, a real bastard. A Portuguese wife who doesn't have a passport from a foreign country can't leave Portugal without her husband's permission. And I don't have a foreign passport. And I can't go to Spain, even if I could go anywhere else, which I can't, because, as Frank would put it, I've been "eighty-sixed" out of Spain. That's why . . .' Her voice dropped. 'That's why Frank had to be brought in on this in the first place . . .'

'You'd better start at the beginning,' Reade said, after a short silence.

CHAPTER FOURTEEN

As Reade walked into Praia da Giz, past orchards of carob trees ripe with fruit, he kept trying to imagine Frank Driscoll here, alive, in Portugal. But for Reade Frank had existed only in the dark world of Greenwich Village bars, complete with juke box and air conditioner, and with no sense of closing time, ever.

The road turned from dry gulch to cobblestone and Reade followed it into the village. The sardine boats could be seen from the road, heading into port once more. In the grounds of the villas gardeners were working, wearing black, wide-brimmed hats. The earth was burnt ochre and the 'smell of Africa' lingered in the air: that was a pure Portuguese smell, made up of burning eucalyptus and donkey shit. The sea was aquamarine, the roofs and chimneys of the buildings were orange. The seamless white of the condominiums at the Giz Bay Club merged in his mind with the white hot passion which Georgia had evoked in him, and which was there now, stirring and obliterating every coherent thought he tried to grasp.

Two dark girls carrying parasols giggled to each other as they passed him; he realized that his face was frozen into its patented commercial smile. They probably thought he was drunk.

He remembered the funeral party at the bridge on the road from Lisbon. The woman pointing at him as he looked at himself in the car mirror. At least he was good at providing amusement for the locals.

He had become entangled in a web of deceit and illusion, only possibly through no fault of his own. Certainly, he thought defensively, no one could blame him for wanting to come to the aid of a lady in distress, even if he did not entirely trust her. And his investment—Frank had screwed it up. Was there anything wrong with picking up a little cash to salvage the Casabranca's losses? And then, undeniably, there was that heady feeling of freedom, that excitement that came from pitting one's talents against a corrupt, meaningless establishment . . .

He had certainly fooled himself about Portugal. That beautiful innocent country of his dreams was an illusion. He had provided the illusion; no one else could be blamed for that. Now he could no longer be spontaneous as he had hoped he could be; as he had stupidly thought the Portuguese were.

There were soldiers on the terrace of the Casabranca. Reade entered his own establishment for the first time, and found Jose Silva there, in the starched and bloused uniform of a major, and apparently in charge.

He had made a command post out of a tall bar stool near the cash register, and he greeted Reade solemnly and invited him with a proprietary air to take the next stool. He spoke briefly to the soldiers who were going through the drawers behind the bar, and they straightened up and left immediately.

'I'm afraid I have bad news for you, Senhor Reade,' he said, in his nasal British accent.

'Bad news?' Reade asked non-committally. He did not really know how he should behave toward Silva. Should he be outraged or calm? Or nervous and subservient? The room was dark and cool, very pleasant. Frank had covered the walls with theatrical posters; he had sent Reade a snapshot of course. Through a graceful archway the dining-room was visible, inviting, with white stucco walls and bright tablecloths.

'Your partner was murdered, sir. He died from a blow to the head. He was already dead when he went into the water. He did not drown. Our tests indicate that he was struck on the head with a pistol.' He looked at Reade carefully. 'Does this surprise you?'

Reade decided to take refuge in nervous sarcasm.

'I didn't think he'd taken a bus from Lisbon to Sagres to jump off a cliff. It would have been more convenient to jump closer to home.'

'Ah,' said Silva politely, nodding his head.

'I see you have gained a sense of humour since yesterday afternoon. Such a thing is often contagious. I assume you caught it, along with the information about the Lisbon bus, from Senhora Portago.'

'Who . . . ?'

'The Irishwoman.'

Silva brought out his pack of Gauloises, and offered them to Reade, who shook his head automatically.

'She is a most friendly woman. I think it is most fortunate that you were able to comfort each other in your so great loss. How should we say . . . partners in misery?' He blew smoke toward the ceiling.

'You're a spy,' Reade said furiously. He did not have to fake his anger. He slid off the stool and walked behind the bar, opening ice chests until he found the one holding beer. He pulled out a bottle and took a long drink. Now on the second of his two days in Portugal he was once more drinking in the morning. Not an auspicious way to begin.

'And you said yesterday you were a translator,' he said. 'You're a lousy spy. You're secret service. You have no reason to spy on me. And you have no reason to search these premises, or even to be here, without a warrant.'

Silva sighed. He had chosen apparently to put on a bored face.

'This is not America, Mr Reade,' he said.

104

'We do not trouble ourselves with charades to protect the so-called rights of criminals, especially in these dangerous times.'

'Hey, who are you calling a criminal? How are you at protecting citizens' rights? My friend was murdered, you said so yourself. That's all I know about it. Just what you told me yourself.'

'Well, that is certainly not the truth,' Silva said gravely. 'You went through Mr Driscoll's papers yourself, yesterday. So you know more than what I have told you. You know that this establishment was in financial difficulties, and you know that your friend flew to London on Tuesday. You know too, apart from what we told you, that he had money—and he did not attain it through legitimate channels.'

'Maybe he borrowed it,' Reade said. He thought of Mowbray.

'That is not impossible,' Silva said, nodding. 'But we have made inquiries, and we have found that your friend had left Portugal regularly in the past two months. He had travelled to Paris, to Seville, to Madrid —twice—and to Zurich, besides his late trip to London. Now . . . why should a penniless man struggling with a failing business take all these holidays? You will tell us that he was perhaps restless?'

Reade took refuge in the beer.

'Senhora Portago . . . your Miss Ryan . . . drove him at least twice to the Spanish border, where he took the ferry to Spain at Vila Real de San Antonio. She waited for him on the Portuguese side. You may or may not be aware that . . . your hostess of last evening is *persona non grata* in Spain? Excuse me.' He slid off the stool, looking rather short by contrast and walked across the room to bark some orders to his soldiers on the terrace.

Reade stared at a poster which advertised the original off-Broadway production of *Waiting for Godot*. A friend of Frank's had worked on the stage crew. That was a symbol of Frank's theatrical connections: a piece of coloured paper cadged through a carpenter. And because Frank was so 'theatrical' Praia da Giz had seen a fancy dress turn-out the night before. He was a little surprised at the bitterness of his thoughts.

Silva came back, followed by a dark soldier carrying a box. One of Frank's book boxes?

'You told us yesterday that Senhor Driscoll was not political,' Silva said.

'That's right,' Reade said. 'He wasn't.' God knew that was no lie.

'Then please explain these.' He snapped his fingers, and his soldier dropped three paperbacks onto the bar from the box. 'Certainly these are subversive,' Silva said, looking at him closely.

Reade looked at the books. *Notes of a Native Son* . . . *For Whom the Bell Tolls* . . . *The Secret Agent*—Joseph Conrad, no less.

He stared at Silva, really at a loss for words now. How could you explain to a Gestapo agent . . .

'And drugs,' Silva said. He reached into the box and pulled out a history of marijuana. A book called *The Beat Generation*.

His expression was triumphant.

'This is absolutely ridiculous,' Reade said.

'Oh? But it is not ridiculous, Senhor Reade. We have here . . .' he tapped the books, 'sufficient grounds to confiscate your property, and to deport you.'

Reade stared at him, horrified.

'And we can place the Portago woman in prison, pending the results of an investigation. It might take a long time, you understand. Eventually there would be a tribunal of inquiry. But you realize this is a political matter, and you are both foreigners . . .'

'You've made your point, Major,' Reade said.

'Now. Tell me the truth. Tell me what you know, and what you think. I want complete co-operation from you.'

'Okay,' Reade said. 'You've talked me into it.'

CHAPTER FIFTEEN

They had moved into the cheerful dining-room, where they could be more comfortable. Silva settled down before a pot of coffee brought by one of his young adjutants. On the table before him lay a pad of paper and a sharpened pencil.

'Georgia told me all about it last night,' Reade said. 'It seems that the money that Frank had on him was part of an advance of expenses for a job. These were primarily travel expenses, but naturally he expected to be recompensed for his trouble. Obviously he could use the money . . . He didn't take me into his confidence about it, you understand. I didn't know a thing about it until last night . . .'

Silva regarded him coldly.

'And the job? What was it?'

Reade poured some coffee into the pottery cup at his place. He noted gratefully that his kitchen seemed well-equipped.

'Well, probably you know already that before she married Portago, Miss Ryan was married to an anti-Franco Spaniard. And that they had a child. That's the crux of her problem, that's why she needed help. The husband had been exiled from Spain; she can't go there either. The ex-husband is in eastern Europe . . .'

'Communist,' Silva said.

'Well, I gather that's true. That's why she divorced him, I think . . .'

Silva continued to stare at him without expression.

'The in-laws are still in Spain—very decent people—but the son is a teenager now, and he's in South Africa. He was living with friends of Georgia's and going to school, but he seems to be a chip off the old block. I'm afraid he's gotten in some trouble with the government there . . . In South Africa . . . He's in prison.'

He drank some coffee. It was delicious.

'Naturally, Georgia wants to get him out, and it's pretty expensive, in South Africa. She has—contacts all over the place—'

'Communist,' Silva said again.

'Well, people both she and her husband know,' Reade said. 'They've passed the hat around . . . The boy's grandparents are naturally concerned too, and they have some money, but their position is a little touchy politically, I'm sure you understand . . .'

Silva's face was like granite.

'Now, any cash—' he gave Silva a significant look, 'any cash that changes hands in a case like this . . . Well, it has to be discreet, naturally. I mean, people have passed the hat in London—and some money has been funnelled to Switzerland . . . It was

109

delicate, it had to be set up, you know. That's where Frank came in. He had to co-ordinate things, visit banks . . . And the money that the in-laws wanted to contribute, it had to be picked up . . . Now Tuesday night Frank got the first instalment, twenty-five thousand pounds. In London, and that's the last Georgia heard from him.'

'Perhaps,' Silva said, 'you could just run through some details. Names, dates . . .'

'Well, damn it,' Reade said irritably. 'Georgia didn't give me all that. She says she does have a name of a contact in Switzerland that she can give you, and she'll try . . .'

'All you have is the name of the husband and his Spanish family . . .'

'And the son . . .'

'And the son. Of course. And I assume the South African friends. And you believe this story?'

'I think it makes sense. It's the kind of thing Frank would love. It's romantic, helping out a woman and a kid. And he'd jump at the chance to run all over Europe on a secret mission.'

He wondered again why he felt so angry with Frank. Poor dead Frank.

'I mean, Georgia needed help,' he said. 'She can't leave Portugal without her husband's consent. He's a real bastard apparently; he cares nothing about someone else's son. He bargained with her . . .'

'So. She is a devoted mother,' Silva said. 'She gave up her rights to the boy completely when she separated from the Communist. But her husband's family keeps in touch with her?'

'Not exactly,' Reade said. 'But everyone keeps in touch with South Africa. And they need each other now. And one thing they all need is money. I don't mean to sound like I'm pleading for her or anything, but she needs money just as Frank needed it. She needs money for a divorce, she's behind in her rent . . . She hasn't got a dime to send anyone for her kid, but she has connections through her former husband, and he has the ability to raise cash.'

Silva shook his head and sighed.

'I'm afraid you're all up to your eyebrows in illegal activities,' he said.

'Well . . .' Reade hesitated. 'Is it illegal to bring money into this country?' he asked.

'No, of course not. But it must be declared. There is an import tax. I would appreciate your frankness here, Mr Reade. I have no time for games.'

Reade leaned over the table, toward Silva; his elbows wrinkled the checked cloth. 'Georgia has asked me to pick up the second payment, Major. In Madrid. The first payment has disappeared, you see; the situation is desperate. The second payment is now fifty thousand pounds sterling. That's one hundred thousand dollars.' He paused impressively. 'Frank was offered ten per cent, you see. And . . . Georgia has empowered me to tell you that she is willing to pay a double tax.'

Silva poured coffee for himself.

'I see,' he said.

'That's five per cent tax,' Reade said. 'It's actually ten per cent, you see . . . Maybe you have a favourite charity.'

Silva drank the coffee.

'Listen,' Reade said. 'Give me back my passport, so I can go to Madrid. I will come back with the money and check in at the border. All you have to do is be there. I get Frank's share of the money, ten per cent there too, and God knows the Casabranca needs it. And Georgia gets the rest and she does what she has to do, and her kid is saved.'

'And what do I do,' Silva said, 'about what she does?'

'Names?' Reade said. 'You want names too? She'll give you two names, she told me to tell you that. Two names. One here and one in Switzerland. That's all she can do.' He dropped his voice. 'But if you watch her after I deliver the money . . .'

'I see,' Silva said. 'I won't say that you do not have a point there. But are you not concerned for yourself? Your partner for some reason died trying to accomplish this apparently simple little operation. I cannot

112

see a possible motivation for murder in what you have told me . . . But could not the same thing happen to you?'

'I don't know what the hell Frank did,' Reade said. 'Who knows who he was talking to on the side? Sure, I suppose there's a gamble, but I'm not Frank . . . Georgia doesn't see how he managed to get himself killed in all this . . .'

He paused. Silva said nothing.

'I count on you to protect me here in Portugal if something's wrong,' Reade said. 'Check out this whole story. I'll take my chances in Spain. After all, Frank was killed here in Portugal, wasn't he? Maybe this will lead us to the guy Frank met in Sagres that night. That's who killed him, in my opinion, someone he was meeting, someone Georgia doesn't know about. Anyway, it may have been a different deal, nothing to do with Georgia. Who knows what Frank was up to? I feel as though I never knew the guy.'

Silva leaned back thoughtfully in his chair, and drummed on the table with his fingertips. 'When would you make the connection in Madrid?' he said at last.

Reade looked at his watch. It was noon on Friday, June 16.

'Sunday night,' he said. 'The eighteenth. That's about fifty-eight hours from now. That's plenty of time, isn't it? I'll drive. I need the car.'

'I will let you know,' Silva said. He rose abruptly. 'I would advise you to avoid the police here. This arrangement is on a somewhat higher level. You will be subject to arrest if you have not been absolutely frank with me.'

Reade nodded. He felt very tense. Apparently Silva was accepting the bribe. Maybe he would just take the money and not even check out Georgia's story. What did it matter after all whether it was true or not? It was the money that mattered—it mattered to all of them. It was the money that made all the difference.

CHAPTER SIXTEEN

Georgia was sunbathing on the patio behind the cliffside villa. Reade walked up, and sank down next to her.

'I've got my passport back,' he said.

She sat up at once. She was wearing a white bikini and huge sunglasses.

'Oh, marvellous!' she said. 'How did you manage it?'

'Well I don't think he thinks I really know anything about all this. I mean, I was on the plane when Frank died, he granted me that himself.'

Her face was wreathed in smiles. 'That's

absolutely smashing,' she said. 'When do you leave?'

'Tomorrow morning. I'll drive. The rendezvous is Sunday night, right? I'll have a day to get my bearings . . .'

She squeezed his hand. 'And you'll be careful. I'd feel so responsible. After Frank . . .'

'Let's just run through this once more, do you mind? You and Frank were the only ones to know about the arrangements for picking up the money in Madrid . . .'

'Right. Frank handled the whole thing personally. He got his orders on the telex at the club, but the man who sent the telex did not even know Frank's precise plans for Madrid. Only Frank knew the times and places and so on.' She took off her dark glasses. Her beauty was partly innocent and vulnerable and, paradoxically, partly world weary. 'The man who telexed Frank is safe. He knows we're going to deliver the package to him before we take our percentage. He probably isn't even interested in what happens in Madrid.'

She leaned back luxuriously. 'And then . . . when it's over . . . I get my divorce, and my Irish citizenship back. And you get the Casabranca's bills paid. And life returns to normal.'

'And your friends from Albufeira?'

'They're in the same spot I'm in. The

money has to be delivered so they can collect their fee.'

'I can't help wondering every once in a while why they don't pick the money up themselves.'

'It's easy to be unpopular in Spain,' she said. She put her glasses back on. 'You're like Frank. You don't understand because you have no history.'

No history. Well, she was right, in a way. He had grown up in a middle-class white-collar Providence neighbourhood, gone to college . . . He knew nothing about this kind of Byzantine European intrigue. The only thing he knew about it was what he had seen in the movies.

'I wish you wouldn't keep things from me,' he said.

'The less you know . . .' she said. 'Haven't you heard that: "What you don't know won't hurt you."'

'It sounds good,' he said. 'It's not true. But you're a tough nut to crack, do you know that?'

She smiled at him. 'It doesn't seem to stop you from trying,' she said.

'I suppose not.'

He leaned toward her, inhaling the coconut smell of her tanning lotion, and kissed her open mouth. He reached for the bikini strap.

'Aren't you afraid we'll be seen?' she asked. 'Gardeners? Neighbours?'

'They're the last thing I'm worried about right now,' he said truthfully.

For the first time that he could remember, he felt no urgency about disrobing. He had no feeling, as he usually did, of a backstage quick-change between the acts; no metronome ticked in his subconscious. He moved slowly and naturally under the hot sun.

They coupled under the cloudless sky and under the eyes, for all he knew, of a dozen people—not the least of whom might be working for Silva. It was slow and easy.

At the climactic moment titles flashed across his mind: *A Night in Lisbon, Odd Man Out, A Coffin for Demetrios, To Die in Madrid* . . . He felt Georgia's nails on his back, and the conjunction of memory and desire and cinematic illusion struck him. He found himself laughing.

'Bloody marvellous,' Georgia said.

CHAPTER SEVENTEEN

'This is a serious matter, Mr Cromwell,' the man from the Banco Hispano said. 'Not to be taken lightly. My government is concerned here. Permission from above,' he pointed impressively to the ceiling, 'was required.'

'I appreciate that, Mr Gonzalez,' Turner

Cromwell said. He adjusted himself in the antique chair, and ran his hand through his shock of unkempt greying hair. 'I appreciate it, and my company appreciates it. We proposed merely a discreet inquiry.'

'Yes, well,' Gonzalez said. 'I tend to agree. There can be no harm in your knowing the history of a moribund account in the name of a non-existent company.'

'So,' Cromwell said. 'There is no "Iberian Sports".'

'False,' the banker said. 'A false company.' He spread his hands palm up above the desk, on which was a collection of marble paperweights fashioned in the shape of animals.

'These are mighty cute,' Cromwell said, picking up a marble elephant.

'My wife,' Gonzalez said, with a smile. 'She likes to collect things.' He put his hand on a thin folder on the blotter in front of him. 'I have everything here. Would you like some coffee before I begin?'

'I think not,' Cromwell said. 'To tell you the truth, my stomach has been acting up a little. Maybe the water.'

'Indeed,' said the banker. 'We all drink it.'

He opened the folder.

'The Iberian Sports account,' he said, 'was opened here at this branch on April 16. The gentleman was named Rivera and was previously unknown to us. Iberian Sports, he said, was involved in the manufacture of sporting goods and in the promotion and sale of lottery tickets. You have seen the lottery vendors on the streets here? Yes, very colourful. At any rate, the nature of his business required that large deposits be made into his account from various locations in Spain and in Europe. He advised us that he would be withdrawing these deposits as soon as they were cleared.'

He looked up at Cromwell and smiled.

'That is not unusual,' he said 'in the lottery business. Prompt payment is of course essential. As long as his deposits were valid, we could have no questions.'

'Did you talk to this man yourself?'

Gonzalez shrugged, and smiled. 'Not I, no.'

'Well . . . do you know who did?'

The banker glanced again at the papers in front of him.

'Yes, of course. But that person is apparently no longer with us, and the laws forbid me to give out information on former employees. My hands are tied there.' He leaned across the desk and dropped his voice significantly.

'But I can tell you that this former employee has been contacted. He remembers Rivera as a well-dressed middle-aged man who spoke Spanish with what he identified as a south-western accent. A . . . drawl, I believe is the word? . . . In the area around Seville, south and west of Seville.'

'I suppose you have no idea then who Rivera is?'

Again the palms-up gesture. 'Ah, Mr Cromwell. Who comes to a bank? Well-dressed middle-aged men. It is impossible.' He leaned once more over the folder. 'But I can tell you that on April 20 we had a deposit in that account of two hundred thousand pesetas. And three days later two-thirds of that money was withdrawn. From here. On May 10, we had a deposit of one hundred and forty thousand pesetas; these were withdrawn immediately from our branch in Merida. A city to the south-west. On June 1 twenty thousand French francs were deposited in a Paris bank, and withdrawn here in pesetas a few hours later. On June 3, five thousand pounds deposited in London—that bank is our agent there—and withdrawn here in French francs.'

'Now forgive me if I ask a foolish question. You understand I'm not familiar with all this. But would there be a delay . . . Is it a little harder to make a withdrawal in a foreign currency?'

'Oh, yes. It was not cleared for forty-eight hours after the request for withdrawal was made. We are always happy to sell pesetas, and Iberian Sports could have instant withdrawal in pesetas. But . . .'

'I suppose nobody noticed the depositor in any of these cases?'

Gonzalez smiled again. He was wearing a black satin tie embossed with the figures of green dancing bears. The wife again, probably.

'But the person or persons who made the withdrawals . . . ?'

'I do not have that information.' Gonzalez looked stern. 'I can tell you the man's name, the date of his birth and his occupation. I cannot tell you anything else, and I must ask you to refrain from making this information public in anyway. We value the custom of World Communications, and I am sure we can rely on you to be discreet. We do not want this name publicized.'

'Well . . . naturally, if you . . . I had no intention of publicizing it anyway, of course.'

'Of course. It is simply routine that I warn you, you understand. The name of the man who withdrew the money, including the deposit from Switzerland on the morning of June 14, is Luis Cordoba Reyes. He was born in 1910 in Seville, and he is a businessman. But that is all I can tell you.'

'Well, now wait a minute,' Cromwell said. 'Rank, name and serial number, eh?' He smiled broadly; the banker did not return his smile. 'But listen, if you know who this fellow is, you can save me a lot of time . . . save my company a lot of time . . . I mean, I'd like to know, for instance, whether you think—'

'Mr Cromwell.' Gonzalez cut him off in a low, sharp voice. 'We are in an area here where perhaps you should tread softly. This man is not unknown, if you see what I mean. I cannot give you any more information, and you would be wise not to press me, and not to press anyone else. Any other Spanish national, I mean. If you wished to inquire from some other agency . . . Say . . .' he paused, and looked into Cromwell's eyes. 'If, for instance, you were to make inquiry from the American intelligence services, no one could blame you.' He looked down again at the file. 'I can tell you that when he left the bank last he had converted the pesetas into bearer notes.'

'Have they turned up?' Cromwell asked. He cleared his throat.

'Yes, as one might expect, they have been cashed at various brokerage offices around Madrid and used to buy stock on Wednesday . . . probably shortly after withdrawal.'

'And the stock was sold immediately.'

Gonzalez shrugged again.

'I think we have told you everything that we can, Mr Cromwell. I hope you are enjoying Madrid? Despite the water.'

Cromwell stood up. 'But can you tell me one thing more . . . Does this fellow have connections in Portugal or Brazil?'

'Oh, I'm afraid I don't know that,'

Gonzalez said. He stood up too, and extended his hand. 'It has been so pleasant to meet you.'

Cromwell skipped the elevator and walked down a broad winding staircase to the main floor. It was noon on Saturday and there were lines of people before the caged tellers. A uniformed guard checked the metal discs in the hands of customers to make sure that they were keeping their proper places in the queue.

He hailed a cab and rode the few blocks to the Ritz. He felt the beginnings of a headache. In his comfortable room, he ordered a Cuba Libre from room service and then placed two long distance telephone calls. After the second, his drink arrived.

He drained it thirstily, and sucked energetically on the lemon he found at the bottom of the glass. Then he lay back on his pillows. He certainly had not wanted to deal with the CIA. But he supposed that now he had no other choice.

CHAPTER EIGHTEEN

The doorman at the Ritz saluted sharply as Michael Reade emerged from the carpeted elegance of the lobby into the noises of the busy Paseo del Prado.

123

Reade crossed the Paseo, pausing for a moment to orient himself in the tree-lined centre island, and then walked to the corner of the avenue called San Jeronimo. He consulted the map of Madrid in his red *Michelin Guide*, and then began to stroll in a leisurely manner up the broad commercial street. Darkness was falling. It was half past eight. His rendezvous was set for ten o'clock.

The street narrowed as it climbed past rows of shops advertising *Farmacias* and *Calzados*. At a round plaza alternate routes to the Plaza Mayor sprouted at forty-five degree angles. There were American-style cafeterias and international newspaper kiosks. Peddlers of lottery tickets haunted the pavement: the lame, the halt and the blind, veterans of the Civil War, hawking their wares in a kind of high monotonous chant, a secular litany.

Reade turned to the left into a narrow street teeming with young people, boys and girls dressed alike in Lacoste shirts and khaki slacks. The *tapas* bars announced their specialties in bold window posters: Gambas, Bocadillas, Langoust. Outside the bars young Spaniards roamed, with glasses of wine or beer in their hands. They carried *tapas*, and, when they were finished eating, carelessly discarded the white napkins in which they were wrapped. The street hummed with laughter and enthusiastic conversation. It was the cocktail hour in Madrid.

Reade went into a bar filled with the smells of onions and fish and the harsh barrelled wine which had soaked into the wooden floors. He settled on a stool at the far end of the zinc bar and ordered beer and shrimp. He took the red book from the inside pocket of his coat; in it was the instruction sheet Georgia had given him. It said:

Enter the Plaza Mayor through the Atocha gate at 10 p.m. Monday, June 19. Carry 1970 Red Michelin Guide to Spain in French. After you pass through the gate take off your coat and then put it on again. Go directly to the left corner: the alfresco Restaurante Jorge. Sit at a table near the entrance, facing the square. Order *jamon de serrano* and *chuletas de ternera*. You will be asked, How are the football scores? And you will answer, Seville is beating Barcelona. Then follow the instructions the contact gives you.

Reade ate the shrimp quickly; it was delicious. He drank his beer and pushed the glass forward to be refilled.

The Plaza Mayor was a massive building, like a fortress, containing theatres, restaurants and offices, built around a paved courtyard the size of many football fields. The inner walls were dotted with arcades holding all kinds of shops. White-jacketed waiters

125

went back and forth busily to tables set up in the courtyard. It was nearly ten o'clock, but the city did not appear to have settled down to dinner yet. The cafes and promenades were filled with people, but the serious eating establishments appeared to be empty. Waiters stood with folded arms in doorways.

Reade stopped under the archway of the Atocha, and removed his jacket. He remembered that he had left the *Michelin Guide* in his pocket, dropped the coat and picked it up and took out the book and then struggled to put his arms back through the damp sleeves.

'*Por favor, Señor*,' said a rasping voice. Reade started; he was very tense. A legless man was standing to the right of him, propped on crutches that raised his shoulders up around his ears. The trousers of his shiny black suit were pinned at the knees. His whole body was not more than four and a half feet long; he wore a black tie painted with the stained, pinkish figure of a girl.

'*Solo cinco pesetas, Señor*,' he croaked. '*Ciegos!*'

He waved his arm; he was clutching a book of green coupons. A lottery ticket salesman.

Michael shook his head sharply, and walked quickly to the far left end of the Plaza: the Restaurante Jorge was large, and prominent. He was the first customer of the evening, so he had no trouble selecting a

126

table, facing the square.

Reade felt better after he had drunk a couple of glasses of the white Rioja, rich from ageing in oak barrels, and eaten the dried mountain ham which was his first course. The tables around him were slowly filling up. After his first glass of wine, he stopped tensing up every time someone, including waiters, approached. After the second glass he began to pretend, without much difficulty, that he was a tourist sampling the glories of Spain. He felt quite happy as he poured his third glass, and barely noticed the ice water dripping onto his trousers from the bottle as he returned it to the bucket. The waiters were not particularly attentive. He held his cold hand against his forehead; the heat of the day was diminishing comfortably.

He looked at the square with appreciation. The roof of the building was a continuous unbroken line against the horizon. Beneath it were three storeys of shuttered windows above the commercial arcades. The arches of the arcades were symmetrical miniature counterparts of the gateways to the city.

'*Por favor, Señor,*' a familiar voice said, close to his ear. 'How are the football scores?'

Reade's eyes met the red-veined ones of the crippled lottery salesman.

His mind was a blank. He thought frantically. It came to him. 'Seville is beating Barcelona,' he said, in a stage whisper. He looked around nervously, but no one appeared to be paying any attention to them. That in itself was a miracle considering the peculiar nature of the courier these people had chosen.

'The package is rather large,' said the salesman, tearing off and handing Reade a block of green coupons. 'Go to the men's room here. It is downstairs and turn to your left. But do not enter—continue along the corridor and go down the next flight of stairs you see there. There is a door at the foot of the stairs, open it, and you will be outside the Plaza, in the Calle de Cuchilleros. There are stone steps on the right which come back up here. You must turn left instead and then take a right into the first narrow alleyway you see. Go to number seventeen in that little *paseo*. I will meet you there in fifteen minutes. Give me one hundred pesetas.'

Reade stared at him. 'The men's room . . .' he said.

'Quick, you fool,' the cripple said urgently. '*Dinero*, what's wrong with you? You must pay for the lottery tickets.' He rubbed the thumb of his left hand against his fingers.

'Oh!' Reade said. 'Sorry.' Embarrassed, he fished in his pocket and came up with a note.

The man smiled; a few of his teeth were missing. '*Bueno*,' he said.

CHAPTER NINETEEN

When he stepped out of the passageway beneath the Restaurante Jorge, Reade found himself in a mean street at the foot of an ancient flight of stone steps. A few doors away two sailors were leaving a grimy cafe; they stumbled noisily up the steps in the direction of the Plaza. The bolt of the door slipped into place behind them, and the Calle de Cuchilleros was momentarily quiet.

He turned left into a street lined with lighted open doorways and the comfort of human company: strolling guitarists from the bars, and the ubiquitous groups of young people. But the street that led off to the right was unmarked and unwelcoming.

It was little more than a corridor carved out of the sandstone of Madrid, a kerbless plane of slick cobblestones winding off into the darkness. There was no light in the buildings, and no indication of such a luxury as house numbers. His leather heels clicked and slipped as he made his way past the low houses, wrinkling his nose against the smell of urine.

At a sharp curve in the road he almost walked into the rough dark walls. He came around the curve to plunge into even deeper darkness; the meagre light from the

Cuchilleros was completely shut out. He stopped, waiting for his eyes to adjust, and listening to the silence, which was broken only by his breathing.

Suddenly a light flickered: about fifty yards ahead he saw the shadow of a crutch protruding from a doorway. As he began to move the light went out, but he retained the image of the light and the crutch on his retina and kept going cautiously forward. The little man's voice spoke, about a foot away.

'Hurry, fool!' he snapped harshly. Then the light came on again: it emanated from a lighter held in the peddler's hand. In spite of the damp stillness of the air, the lighter flame flickered madly about, projecting ominous shadows everywhere, and casting bands of light onto the man's repellent face.

'You must tell your employer that *El Cordero Pequeno* does not like to deal with amateurs.'

'I'm sorry,' Reade said shortly. 'I just came to pick up a package.'

'And where is the other, the serious one? He liked to drink . . .' The flame flared dangerously near the man's mouth, almost enveloping his nose. Hanging incongruously over his shoulder, outside the crutch, was a smart long-strapped leather bag; it glowed expensively in the light.

'He had an accident,' Reade said.

'Ah, you have a dangerous calling. Like the

130

war. I lost these in the war.' He gestured toward his legs. 'They sent another man with two legs to replace me. They will replace you, too, as you replaced your friend . . .'

'Listen,' Reade said. 'I'd like to get this over with.'

'Oh, you are impatient,' the peddler said. 'Your friend was not so impatient. But perhaps he loitered too long, eh?'

The light went out suddenly, and Reade felt a rough hand on his arm, and then smooth leather in his hands.

'Put it on your shoulder like the tourists do,' the peddler said.

Reade slipped his arm through the strap. The bag was heavy.

'*Adios*,' the man said. Reade's eyes had adjusted sufficiently to the darkness so that he could distinguish the outlines of the figure on crutches, who said, 'You return to Cuchilleros, I go the other way.'

'Wait a minute,' Reade said. 'This man who came before me. He had an accident, as I said. Can you tell me anything about him that could have caused that accident? I don't want to have an accident myself . . .'

'I have no time to stand here now, friend,' the man said testily. He turned away, and spoke over his shoulder. Suddenly, bright lights flashed against the barred and shuttered windows across the alley from them.

For a moment time froze, and then gears

shifted and an automobile engine made a rising whining noise. The headlights were coming from behind a curve in the road, from the direction in which the Spaniard was heading. Reade shouted; his words were lost in the roar as the car rounded the curve and bore down upon them. The peddler, caught in the glare, turned on his crutches and began to move desperately, crablike, away from the lights. The car almost filled the street: not more than an inch separated the fenders from the walls.

Reade leaped for one of the barred windows, the shoulder bag swinging at his side. He grabbed the top bar with his right hand and pulled himself up with his left; he could feel rust against his palms. His toes caught the window sill, and he pressed his knees as far as he could into the cracks made by the vertical bars. His backside protruded into the street, just above the widest part of the low-slung car. He gritted his teeth, his whole body strained, and waited for the impact.

The car struck the legless man; the crutches flew into the air. There was a crunch, a sickening scream, and the awful tearing sound of metal on stone. The car screeched to a halt. The lights went out, the street went black again. Then the back-up lights went on. There was another crunch of metal; the rear of the car must have hit part of a building. The gears ground into forward again, there was more grinding, and the motor painfully wound out in reverse. Reade released his grip, and slipped and fell onto the cobblestones. He got up quickly and scrambled away from the noise and the lights. He came around a corner, slipped again and crunched his knuckles painfully against a wall.

There was another crashing noise. Then a shot rang out. A bullet ricocheted from one side of the alley to the other. He ran hunched over so far that his fingers touched the cobblestones. Then he was past the turning and had emerged into a busy street. It was amazing that life was going on normally then; people were dining, looking into shop windows.

Someone had tried to kill him. He thought suddenly that he was a week short of his birthday. Someone had tried to kill him before his thirty-third birthday. The silent dark alley had almost been his grave.

He plunged through the street into the square. His hands were scraped and sore; he had torn the knee of his trousers. Trembling, he hailed a taxi.

CHAPTER TWENTY

'It's a pretty interesting story,' Mr Browne said. 'I don't mind telling you you've come forward at a time when we're looking at interesting stories like this.'

He sat down in a brown armchair and crossed his legs. Turner Cromwell noted with interest that all Mr Browne's clothes were brown, too: suit, socks, shoes, necktie. Even his shirt was light brown.

'I like to think that people like you trust us enough to come to us,' Mr Browne went on. 'That's what we're here for, after all. To help.'

'I thought so,' Cromwell said, nodding. 'I thought you could help. If anyone could identify this Reyes fellow you could.'

'Oh, sure,' Mr Browne said. He closed his eyes. 'Luis Cordoba Reyes. *El Cordero Pequeno*. The Little Lamb.' He opened his eyes again. 'That's what he called himself. Everybody in Madrid knew him. He lost his legs in the Civil War—on Franco's side, of course. Fighting Communists. Franco gave him a medal. He had a lot of friends, Mr Cromwell. I mean, the little people loved him. Well, he was a hero.'

'I see,' Cromwell said.

'Sure, you do. Guy had no legs, fought in

the war. It was a lucky thing for him his side won, right?' Mr Browne went off into a wheezy laugh. Cromwell managed a weak smile.

'Of course,' Browne said, 'he had to live. He did all kinds of things. Took bets on bullfights . . . worked the lottery . . . He had connections. You know. He was pretty political. Well, that was a Communist shell that blew his legs off. He had friends in high places.'

'So that's why the bank wouldn't tell me anything about him yesterday?'

'Right! He circulated. He dressed cheap and sold his own lottery tickets; he hung around with the bookies and the ticket scalpers at the Plaza de Toros. He kept his eye on things. Boy, he was a real eyesore.'

'Was,' Cromwell said.

'Well, yes. That's the funny part of it. Here you come asking about him, and now this morning he's in the papers.'

Browne pulled a folded tabloid from the pocket of his brown jacket. 'It's on the third page, but what the hell. He had an accident last night. Hit and run.'

'Did anyone see—'

'In an alley off the Plaza Mayor. No one around. Deserted alley.'

'Could they find—'

'Rented car. It was dumped. And the guy who rented it had used a stolen Brazilian passport. It's pretty sad. Poor cripple. The papers think the guy was drunk. The driver, not the cripple.' He dropped the newspaper on the arm of his chair. 'He's going to have a military funeral. And they're lighting candles in all the churches . . . Well, he's going to be missed, Mr Cromwell, no doubt about it. Take the Emergency Colonial Relief Fund, for instance. He handled a lot of their contributions. Who knows? Maybe he was carrying a bundle of contributions last night. A lot of people are going to feel just terrible about this.'

'You have no idea who killed him, do you?' Cromwell asked, randomly.

'How could we know? He was very popular, Mr Cromwell, but naturally anyone in business like that makes enemies. Some people didn't like his politics, but a lot of other people may not have liked his business methods. Who knows? I don't think Franco's people are busted up over this. His friends were to the right of Franco.'

'Do you know who his friends were? Could you tell me anything about his dealings?'

'No, I can't,' Browne said soberly. 'But I did find something you might be interested in.'

He took out some folded papers from his inside coat pocket and handed them to Cromwell. They were copies of a file on an American citizen named Frank Xavier

136

Driscoll, who had been operating a bar in Portugal, and whose body had washed up on the Algarve a few days earlier. A small photograph was clipped to the papers. Cromwell looked at it closely.

'You think this is our Mr Eliot,' he said.

'Well, he fits the description. I can look into that with you, Mr Cromwell.'

Browne stretched out luxuriously in the armchair.

'An American citizen, washed up on the beach so to speak . . . And you represent World Communications. Hell, I don't think there's a person in Washington who has a word to say against World Communications.'

'I appreciate that, Mr Browne,' Cromwell said.

'Hell,' Mr Browne said, 'call me Sam.'

CHAPTER TWENTY-ONE

Reade drove past fields of emaciated cattle that made him think of bleached skulls; the occasional tree was twisted like a dervish between the baked earth and the blinding sky. He drove through plains, mesa, plains again, and then the road rose into the stony hills of the Estramadura.

On the seat next to him was the leather shoulder bag. On the back seat was a large earthenware jug which he had purchased on the side of the road near a town called Guadalupe, and into which he had stuffed what he thought was probably the equivalent of nine hundred thousand dollars. The other hundred thousand, which was the amount he had been expecting to get, and which he had told Silva he would be carrying, was still in the leather bag, covered with some paperback books and other travelling gear. The mouth of the jug was stuffed with newspapers.

He was still trying to forget the sounds he had heard in that alley in Madrid: the crunch of metal on stone and flesh; that scream . . . He still felt hunted. Probably the way Frank had felt . . . But he, Reade, expected to live to remember it all.

Badajoz was the last town in Spain; none of them had offered much relief from the hot plain. Whether it was Talavera, Trujillo or Merida, the road ran through the same dusty outskirts, through jumbles of bicycles, past broken-down gas stations and gypsy camps sprawled near foul stagnant streams.

It was early Monday afternoon when he arrived, parched and grimy, at the border.

The line of cars was being inspected by a civilian Customs man overseen by an armed member of the *Guardia Civil*. The Customs officer was very young, and looked stupid. He looked for a long time at Reade's passport and insurance papers. The trooper from Franco's elite corps noticed the delay and moved closer, his tri-cornered leather hat throwing a shadow over the other man's face. He said something to the civilian and the man nodded and returned the passport reluctantly to Reade. Then he removed a long piece of chalk from his pocket and gestured with it at Reade to get out of the car.

Reade came unstuck with a popping noise from the hot car seat.

The officer pointed to the trunk of the car.

Reade opened it. His suitcase lay inside, along with a hand-carved wooden chess set and a bottle of Fundador. He had bought them both the day before in Madrid so that he would look like a tourist.

The Customs official made a quick slashing mark on the suitcase with his chalk.

'And inside?' he said, in English. He pointed to the interior of the car.

'Books,' Reade said. His voice squeaked. He cleared his throat and tried it again. 'Just some books and film.'

'And the bag?'

Reade stared at him blankly.

'The bag,' the man repeated impatiently. 'The bag. Spanish leather, no? From Madrid?'

'Oh. Sure. Yes, of course.'

The Customs man leaned inside the car and ran his hand over the bag. 'Spanish leather,' he said. 'A good bargain for you, no?' He scrawled on the bag, slammed the door and moved away with a wave of his hand. Apparently to him the jug was simply a natural part of the landscape. Reade got back into the car, but it was not until the trooper in the three-cornered had gestured him on that he started the car and drove off.

Apparently he had made it.

He accelerated toward the Portuguese Customs House, along a broad empty four-lane road under an umbrella of plane trees. He felt as if he had broken into the open on a touch-down run. He was euphoric. The horrors of Madrid were momentarily forgotten: he had made it, he had pulled it off. Now all he had to do was check in with Silva on the Portuguese side, pay the 'tax' and take the rest of the money to Georgia. She could make her delivery, take her share, and it would all be over. Silva would no longer be interested in her: his interest would follow the money. That was the deal.

Of course, there was that extra money. Why had it been in the bag? Was that why he had almost been killed himself? But maybe the murder there had nothing to do with him or Georgia; it could have been some kind of gang vendetta. How could those people in Madrid know anything about him, and why would they even want to kill him? The driver of the car probably didn't even know who he was; it was dark in that alley and he had turned away from the lights . . . Anyway now he was over the border and the PIDE would protect him, even if anyone were after him. But the money . . .

Reade pulled the car up beside a large black Mercedes with official-looking plates. He hoisted the bag onto his shoulder, got out of the car and followed Silva, who had materialized from the chaos outside the Customs House, into a small office.

A door was open into a larger, more comfortably furnished adjoining room. Silva sat on the desk, favourite perching spot, apparently, and gestured Reade to the straight-backed armchair in front of it. Before he sat down, Reade leaned over and dropped the bag on the desk next to Silva. 'Here it is,' he said. He felt dust in his throat and suddenly began to cough violently.

'I was sorry to hear your news on the phone last night,' Silva said, frowning.

'You should have been there,' Reade said. He leaned back against the tall chair, and rested his eyes for a moment. 'And waiting to get through to you on the phone was interminable.'

Silva turned his attention to the bag. He got up and moved around to the back of his desk and, standing up, dumped out the contents of the bag. 'Pesetas,' he said, and began to count them.

'Have you found out anything?' Reade

said. He was still coughing a little.

'Not much,' Silva said. He did not look up. Something about him made Reade nervous.

'I almost got killed last night,' he said weakly.

Silva's tone was dry. 'So you told me,' he said. 'And so did you also tell Senhora Portago?'

'Well, I spoke to her, yes. What's wrong with that? After all, she's certainly the one most concerned here. I didn't dwell on the unpleasantness. I just wanted to set her mind at rest about the money.'

He could still hear the shock in Georgia's voice when he told her over the phone about his close call in Madrid. She certainly sounded shocked; she could not possibly have known about the danger that had awaited him.

'Well, Mr Reade,' Silva said, 'could you not set my mind at rest as well?'

'What do you mean?'

'You know quite well what I mean. You will set my mind at rest by telling me the truth, which you have not done up to this point.'

'The truth . . .'

'The truth, yes. We have made inquiries, you see, and your story is false. The Irishwoman's son has been arrested now and then on minor charges, but he is not at the moment in prison, nor is he in danger of

142

being arrested. And his loving grandparents, the in-laws of Senhora Portago, are dead, did you not know that?'

Reade's mind was a blank. He said weakly, 'That was not my understanding.'

'Not your understanding! Then the woman has deceived you?'

'Oh, no, I . . . No.'

'Then you have conspired with her to deceive me?'

Reade was at a total loss. It was he who had concocted the story of the imprisoned boy—or rather had embellished Georgia's reasons for not being able to travel to Spain, in order to ensure Silva's co-operation. Now what could he say? The truth would be deadly for Georgia: that she and Frank had been hired to smuggle and launder illicit profits for a prominent Portuguese citizen who wished to evade paying taxes . . .

Georgia would go to prison, the Casabranca would be permanently closed, his investment would be lost . . . and he himself . . . They could put him in prison, too. He had nine hundred thousand undeclared dollars in that jug in the car. One hundred thousand dollars had seemed like a containable, almost *innocent* amount. But now . . . a million . . . He was playing in a bigger—and chillier—league than he had imagined. He felt a physical need to go to the window and look to see if they were searching his car.

'There must be some mistake,' he said. 'I need to talk to Georgia. It's some innocent mistake, I'm sure . . .'

Silva had separated the money into two piles, one large and one small. He dumped the larger pile back into the bag. He called, and a uniformed Customs officer appeared through the door to the adjoining room. Silva gave him the smaller pile of money and took some kind of paper from him. He wrote on it and handed it to Reade.

'Here is your receipt,' he said, 'for the importation tax on the money you have brought into Portugal. Do you want to count it?'

Reade leapt to his feet; the chair tipped over behind him onto the concrete floor. 'Wait a minute!' he said. 'What's going on here?'

Silva was unruffled. 'Merely a tax formality,' he said.

'But . . . what about Georgia? And . . . you know . . . the . . . I wanted protection, you promised me . . .'

Silva looked at him pityingly. 'But you cannot go to Senhora Portago,' he said. 'She seems to have disappeared during the night. And the Casabranca . . . It is under the jurisdiction of Captain Batista, surely you knew that? In any case, I no longer wish to have any further dealings with you or with any of your friends. Take the money, you have paid the tax, and go. I will not ask how you came by it.'

He walked over and opened the door to the car park.

'Goodbye, Senhor Reade,' he said.

Reade stumbled out onto the gravel, the bag hanging over his shoulder. A chauffeur sat in the front seat of the black Mercedes, smoking a cigarette. Reade thought he gave him a contemptuous look.

Now what? Where was Georgia? Had she in some way betrayed him? Or did she think he had betrayed her? Or both? She was gone . . . His stomach felt strange. Maybe she was dead. Murder seemed to be everywhere. If people disappeared perhaps they were dead. Frank had disappeared . . .

What was he going to do with all this money?

And Silva had not taken his share.

He turned south toward Giz. He had nowhere to go except the Casabranca. It was home.

*   *   *

Inside the Customs House Sam Browne emerged from the large adjoining office, with Turner Cromwell looming behind him.

'Very good, Major,' Browne said to Silva. 'Very convincing.'

Silva shrugged. 'I think he is simply a

145

pawn. He knows nothing. He went into a panic.'

'Yes, but he bothers me,' Cromwell said. 'How does he end up with the money? By all the rules he should be dead.'

Browne turned on him jovially. 'Well, now don't be so morbid, friend,' he said. 'They just missed him somehow. Dumb luck. For us, too. If we stay with him they're bound to come after him sooner or later. And we'll have front row seats.'

'Just like a bullfight,' Cromwell said.

'Well, they don't kill the bull in Portuguese bullfights,' Browne said, winking at Silva. 'At least not in the ring. I hear they slaughter him under the stands after the fight is over.'

'He's going back to Praia da Giz,' Cromwell said thoughtfully.

'He has nowhere else to go,' Silva said. 'It has been a pleasure dealing with you, gentlemen.'

'We'll keep in touch,' Browne said.

'Oh, by all means.'

Browne climbed into the Mercedes, and asked the chauffeur, 'Is it there?'

The chauffeur nodded. 'In a jug in the back seat.'

Cromwell smiled. 'I wonder if Silva would like to have the tax on *that*?'

'Well,' Browne said. 'I'm not going to worry about it.'

Georgia's villa was deserted. Reade looked in the closets, threw back the bedclothes, emptied the wastebaskets. On the kitchen table, in plain view, was a grocery list. On the bottom of the list in large letters Georgia had written two words: Cold Stove, and surrounded them with curlicues.

Drained, Reade sank down onto Georgia's bed and lay there, his heart beating like a bass drum. Here he was in a lonely house at the end of a dirt trail. Here he was, with the money. He didn't even know why he had it.

Wearily, he dragged himself off the bed and down to his car and drove to the Casabranca, where he sat on the balcony overlooking the beach and drank a few glasses of Fundador. There seemed to be a hole at the centre of his being, which he might be able to fill up with alcohol. He drank until he was numb.

He fell asleep at last in Frank's bed, with the jar of money next to him. He heard the sounds of revelry from the Giz Bay Club, and thought dreamily about the picture of Frank and Philip Vandermint in Red Sox caps.

The Cold Stove League.

CHAPTER TWENTY-TWO

Philip Vandermint was staying in a modern back street hotel in Lagos. On Tuesday morning, Reade found him in his room packing a dufflebag. A mound of wrinkled clothing lay on the unmade bed. There was a litter of scuba diving gear on the floor. Draped over a chair was the army uniform Vandermint had worn on the night of the wake.

'You taking a trip?' Reade asked. He felt insecure as an interrogator and he knew that his attitude betrayed this.

'Yeah,' Vandermint said. 'What's your problem? Why don't you have a drink?' He poured vodka and orange juice into a squat tumbler.

'It's a little early.'

'Early?' Vandermint looked surprised. 'Early for what?'

He had a point. Reade drank the mixture and felt a little better.

'But you're leaving town,' he said, trying again.

'That's right,' Vandermint said. 'I'm going to Boston, as a matter of fact. There's a three game series with the Yankees this week at Fenway Park. The pennant race is getting into gear.'

'You're only going for the week?'

'Oh, I don't know. My family has a place in Maine. It's empty until August—I may hang around there for a while. I usually don't get back here until September, when the cheap English package tours stop.'

'Where do you spend August?'

'It depends,' Vandermint said, stuffing clothes into the bag. 'Everyone is out of town in Paris and New York in August. I don't like crowds.'

'How do you keep in touch with the will of the masses?' Reade asked. He was aware that he sounded stupidly sarcastic.

Vandermint looked at him briefly. '*They* don't leave town in August,' he said. 'The bourgeoisie do. You can reach the proletariat any time.'

It was impossible to tell whether Vandermint was serious. He did not look annoyed, and his voice was pleasant. Reade decided to take a shot in the dark.

'How do you feel about Madrid in June?' he asked. 'Say last Sunday night. Say the Plaza Mayor.'

'How do I feel about it?' Vandermint glanced at him again. 'I don't get you, buddy.'

'Were you in Madrid last Sunday night?'

'No, was I supposed to be? I played soccer here with the Trades Union League. Did you think you saw me in Madrid?'

'Were you with Georgia?'

Vandermint laughed. 'What are you doing, checking up on her? Don't worry about it; we barely speak. She's not crazy about my politics and I sure as hell don't care for hers. She's the worst kind of unreconstructed capitalist. Revenge against her husband for leaving her maybe. I hear he was a revolutionary type.'

'She disappeared yesterday,' Reade said.

Vandermint poured some more vodka and orange juice.

'Oh, yeah?' he said. 'No kidding.' He didn't look particularly interested.

Reade took another drink. There was a soccer ball under the bed. He decided to try another tack.

'I've been meaning to ask you,' he said, 'about the Cold Stove League.'

Vandermint threw the empty orange juice container into a waste basket and began to roll up a pair of jeans.

'Where'd you hear about that?' he said.

'You mentioned it,' Reade said. 'At the club just before . . . before Frank turned up. You said something about—I should ask Frank what it was like to play games in the Cold Stove League . . . Something like that.'

'Oh, it was a kind of joke,' Vandermint said. 'The winter here is pretty bad, you know. Did Frank tell you about it?'

Reade shook his head.

'Well, he sure talked about it a lot. This isn't the place to spend the winter, you know. These buildings aren't strong on heat; the chimneys are mostly decoration. If you're poor you wear a lot of clothes. It rains a lot and it's damp. Goes right through you.' He poured himself another drink and filled Reade's glass. 'And there's no one here. Sort of like Paris in August, you know? I kind of like that. I'm an off-season character.'

'So?'

'So that's why I'm a charter member of the Cold Stove League. It's made up of off-season characters. You know. Frank, and me . . . a couple of others. We used to drink *medronho* in a dive downtown and try to keep warm . . . Mowbray too, you know him.'

'Mowbray doesn't like crowds either?'

'He doesn't like his wife, pal. Where she goes, he doesn't. So last winter she went to Tahiti. He stayed here.'

They drank in silence.

'Frank and I were talking baseball. It reminded me of the Hot Stove League, all of us hanging around. You know, off-season. Owners and managers hang around and make trades and plan for the next season. Like sitting around a Franklin stove in a general store in New Hampshire, shooting the breeze and playing cards or whatever. I suppose they all go to Florida and hang around a pool, but I liked the idea of the Hot Stove. So Frank said our league was the Cold Stove League, all freezing our asses off hanging around here. Frank was funny, wasn't he?'

'He could be,' Reade said.

'Yeah, he could be. Poor guy, he came here with the ultimate bourgeois fantasy: warm beach, rich women, English gentlemen . . . And instead here he was, a charter member of the Cold Stove League. It seemed funny at the time anyway. He started getting into the sauce pretty heavy there . . .' He tossed his glass aside and got up. 'That's another reason I'm splitting,' he said, zipping the bag closed. 'I want to dry out a little. There's a lot going on in the States; I need some distraction.'

Reade got up and moved to the door.

'So what'd you come here for in the first place?' he said.

Vandermint looked at him and smiled.

'I came for the waters,' he said.

'Oh, okay,' Reade said. 'See you around.'

'Hey,' Vandermint said. 'Don't go away mad. I thought you liked the Bogart routine. Frank did it all the time. You know that Neil Young song, "Everybody Knows This is Nowhere"?' He launched into it suddenly, in a surprisingly sweet, mellow voice.

'Sure,' Reade said, surprised. 'I know it.'

'Well, that's where it's at,' Vandermint said. 'In a certain mood, this is it for me. Everybody knows this is nowhere.'

CHAPTER TWENTY-THREE

Reade walked down a cobbled hill to a busy cafe in the centre of Lagos, and ordered another vodka and orange juice. The waiter brought him gin and grapefruit juice. He was surprised to find that he did not really care what the drink tasted like; he was already drunk. Well, so what? It was as good a thing to do as any other, under the circumstances. He looked across the square, where he could see his Volkswagen in the municipal parking lot. That dreary little bug was carrying almost a million dollars. And he had got it, through his own efforts, and it belonged to him now, apparently; he could do what he wanted with it. He was a dreary little man with a dreary little car with a million dollars in it. He ordered another drink.

The only problem was, he didn't know what to do with it. He couldn't even let anyone know he had it. Georgia, it all revolved around Georgia. If only she would come back. Why hadn't she got in touch? It was taking too long. It was scary.

She might have set him up for that kill in the first place.

Maybe she had found out he was collaborating with the PIDE. But now the PIDE didn't seem to want anything to do with him either.

But they didn't know about his million dollars.

It was kind of funny, really. All dressed up and no place to go. Why did Georgia write 'Cold Stove' at the bottom of her shopping list? Was she thinking out loud? Was she talking to Vandermint at the time? What did Cold Stove matter, to her, in June? It just didn't fit. Vandermint was a jerk anyway. And probably a liar. He wasn't going to Boston.

But it was hard to imagine him driving that car in that narrow alleyway.

He decided it would be wise to eat something. He ordered a *Bifstek Portuguese* and a bottle of red wine. He wanted a half-bottle but the waiter brought a bottle. Of course he didn't have to drink all of it. Then again, he had all the time in the world. The noon sun was directly over the square; he sat comfortably in the shade of an orange and blue *Sumo Real* umbrella. He thought he might as well pretend he was on vacation.

There were holidaymakers all around him: Germans in cowboy hats, badly sun-burned English families wearing sandals and cotton socks and ordering frugally to the obvious disdain of the waiters. A group of urchins were gathered around a table where four Japanese tourists sat, laden with cameras. Occasionally waiters shooed the children away, but they returned to stare in fascination. Reade drank his wine and forced himself to eat some of the pickled vegetables garnishing the casserole of cubed steak.

One of the children detached himself from the group, and came to Reade's table. With a jolt Reade recognized Big Tony. He leaned conspiratorially toward Reade, although his chin touched the top of the table.

'Senhor Miguel de Casabranca,' the boy said, 'I have a message from Senhora Ryan. My aunt is her maid. She tell her tell me tell you. She at Hotel Real, Rua Alegria, Lisbon. *Amanha*. Tomorrow morning. She say "Tell him remember Irish wake." Okay, man?'

'Far out,' Reade said.

'Far fucking out,' the kid echoed.

'Have some vino,' Reade said. *'Amanha!'*

'Of all the gin joints in the world, she had to walk into mine,' he added.

He felt euphoric, but wary. It was interesting that she should suddenly surface. There was always the money. Irish wake or no Irish wake. She wanted that money. There was really no reason in the world to trust her.

In a sense she had walked out on him, hadn't she? Given him a bad time. Maybe he should tell Silva about it. There might be something waiting for him in Lisbon that he didn't expect. Silva was a form of protection. Well, he was, wasn't he? He had kept his end of the bargain. More than she had done, so far anyway.

He crossed the square to the Camera Municipal. To his surprise his knees buckled. He straightened quickly and began to walk with wide steps in order to keep his balance. It occurred to him that he was swaggering. Like Frank? Frank swaggered. He had not realized before that Frank was trying to keep his balance because he was usually drunk.

Silva was not available. The only other person Reade could think of was Batista, and that would be a really self-defeating encounter. There was no way he was going to unburden himself to Batista.

He went back to the cafe, and had a coffee. It didn't do much for him, so he drank a couple of Fundadors. The brandy levelled his equilibrium and clarified his thoughts.

He ought to talk to somebody; somebody ought to know he was going to Lisbon at Georgia's request. Silva was the person, but Silva was not around. He could give someone a message to Silva; then it would be all right. Who was reliable?

Not Vandermint. He was leaving anyway. Clive Mowbray. Sort of a Colonel Blimp, but he seemed like a reasonable sort of guy. After all, he had lent money to Frank. He was really the only one who had offered help. Georgia wasn't too helpful, rushing off like that without a word, and letting him beat his brains out here like that . . .

Mowbray's house was built like a battleship; it radiated solidarity. Mowbray himself was standing on his neatly trimmed lawn, playing a solitary game of croquet. The scene looked like a parody of English country-house life.

The Englishman struck one heavy ball against another. The latter rolled through the wicket as he reached for a tall clear drink with a slice of lime.

'I say, hello,' Mowbray said happily. 'Have a pint or something.'

'I've spent the morning at the Abrigo,' Reade said ruefully.

'Good! You're picking up the local customs. Get pissed in the morning; sleep it off in the afternoon. Come along.'

They went into the house through a roomy entrance hall and then into a large dark room, filled with overstuffed furniture. A tray with bottles and an ice bucket stood on a mahogany table.

'What'll it be?'

'Fundador.'

'Have a cognac. Easier to handle.'

Reade sank back into a massive armchair. He was a little sleepy.

'Listen,' he said. 'You know Georgia Ryan?'

'Ah,' Mowbray said approvingly. 'Lovely woman.' He picked up a violin from a side table and began to pluck at the strings.

'Well,' Reade said, 'I went to Spain for her. On business. I came back with a package for her. But she wasn't here when I got back. I spoke to Silva . . .'

'What, Jose Silva? Our local PIDE watchdog? Did you really? Asked him to locate Georgia, what a good idea.'

'Yes, I'm concerned . . . I was concerned about Georgia's safety. But this morning I found out she was all right; she's in Lisbon.' He leaned forward, the cognac lurching around inside him. 'I couldn't find Silva . . . This morning. I couldn't find Silva this morning. So listen, will you see him when you can, and tell him I am meeting Georgia at the Hotel Real, Rua Alegria . . .'

'Oh, yes I know it. It's a charming place.' He tucked the instrument under his chin, flourished the bow, and tentatively stroked the opening bars of *April in Portugal*.

'I hope you can see him before eight tomorrow morning . . . Otherwise . . .' he tried to think. 'Otherwise maybe Batista . . .'

'What, that swine? You mean you want the local constabulary to rush off to Lisbon after you . . . ?'

Put that way, it did seem sort of silly.

'No,' Reade said slowly. Probably he should not have had so much to drink this morning. It made it hard to concentrate. 'They could tell the police in Lisbon, though. They could—watch the hotel around eleven in the morning. So there isn't any trouble.'

'Well,' Mowbray said. 'I don't know what you mean by trouble, and it all sounds most confusing, but you can rely on me, old man. I'll give Silva your message. I can't think that it would be necessary for me to talk to Batista.'

'Good,' Reade said. He heaved himself up. 'I think . . . a siesta would be the ticket . . .'

'Oh, definitely the ticket, old dear. Just toddle on back and sleep it off. You look a bit green around the gills.'

He walked Reade politely out of the house, and back onto the spreading lawn, trailing fiddle and bow beside him like weapons held in reserve.

'Thanks a lot,' Reade said. 'I really appreciate this. Oh—and by the way, would you mention this to Silva? Just the words, "Cold Stove". I don't know what it is, but he might.'

'Right,' Mowbray said. 'Cold Stove. And Hotel Real, Rua . . .'

'Alegria.'

'Rua Alegria, eleven a.m. Lisbon, of course. I think I'll go back in and write all this down while I remember it.'

'Thanks a lot,' Reade murmured, and walked off, as firmly as he could.

'Good luck,' Mowbray called after him good-naturedly. 'Not to worry.'

Just before he managed to fumble the key

into the ignition and start the VW, Reade heard Mowbray playing *Lady of Spain* and looked back to see the bulky Englishman wielding his bow gaily from under the portico. Reade's mind reeled: 'Lady of Spain, I adore you,' he found himself half-singing, half-chanting, under his breath. 'Adore you adore you adore you . . .'

CHAPTER TWENTY-FOUR

Hans Hauptmann sat sipping Evian water and waiting for his stomach to calm down. The first-class section was virtually empty, as was usually the case on the Wednesday morning flight from Zurich to Lisbon. He was regretting finishing off the *Carbonnades à la Flamande* the evening before, and his digestion was not helped by the various messages he had received in the past few days.

The Thursday rendezvous at the Cold Stove had been moved up to Wednesday, today, apparently; so the woman had telexed anyway. Naturally he had wished to confirm her telex but he had not been able to reach anyone for confirmation. A telex was not like a spoken message, of course; there was no spontaneity there, no room for nuance: a tone of voice a choice of words, a significant pause

. . . Portugal was a mistake entirely; they did not have a reliable telephone system. Putting calls through required hours of waiting.

It was interesting that the woman was making communication. Could she have clearance to do this? She might be easier to deal with than the man if in fact she were speaking for him . . .

He shifted in his seat, and his foot hit the small suitcase on the floor. Soon that would be bulging with money . . . The possibilities were enticing. After all, Hauptmann knew rather more about the operation than he was probably intended to know . . . And after all, the concept and half the financing had been provided by Hauptmann. The agent was no longer a factor. The brokers in Madrid had been taken care of. Who was more entitled to the profits of the Cold Stove League than he, Hans Hauptmann? He couldn't think of anyone.

CHAPTER TWENTY-FIVE

Reade got out of the diesel-propelled taxi and looked around. The Hotel Real was situated south-west of the broad, tree-lined Avenida de Libertade, near the peak of one of Lisbon's seven hills. The front of the hotel was neat but unremarkable, and the street in which it was located simply a wall of stone buildings. The air was thick with the exhausts of cabs and motorbikes. Parked a little way up the incline of the hill was the shiny black Mercedes sedan with official plates; it looked very like the one which had stood outside the border office near Badajoz. As he stared at it, the doorman emerged from the revolving door and ushered him into the hotel.

Did the presence of the Mercedes mean that Mowbray had got in touch with Silva? He carried his bag, stuffed with the overflow of currency which he had been given in Madrid.

The lobby was small but furnished with comfortable leather furniture and deeply carpeted.

'Yes, sir,' the desk clerk said in English. He nodded politely to him. 'May I help you? Oh, Senhora Portago. Of course. She is in two twenty one.'

Room 221 was directly across from the elevator.

Reade, alone in the silent, plush corridor, waited a moment, then tapped on thc door. He heard a bolt being drawn, and saw Georgia staring at him through the partly opened door. Then she opened the door all the way, without speaking, and he entered the room.

There was an awkward pause as they faced each other. Reade had not found his hangover enhanced by the three hours of driving he had just done.

He found himself looking at Georgia with dull resentment. Why on earth was he here, and involved in this crazy thing, whatever it was, at all?

'So you made it through Customs,' she said, 'and you had no trouble in Giz.' He nodded, looking at her.

'I'm so terribly sorry,' she said.

He dropped the bag on the floor and began to empty his pockets on the white bedspread. 'Here it is,' he said. 'I believe it's ten times what you expected.'

She sank onto the bed. She was wearing a dark pants suit; it was rather tailored, for her.

'Actually,' she said, 'I did expect it. I didn't tell you how much there was because I didn't want to scare you off. I wanted you in this with me. And I wanted you safe, of course.'

'Safe? Like Frank, maybe? How much did he think *he* was picking up?'

'Oh, don't be an ass,' she said. 'That was an entirely different operation. Frank stole that money. Or rather he arranged for it to be stolen . . . He didn't have any money on him; only his allowance for expenses. And no one murdered him. It was an accident . . . I know it was an accident. That's why . . .' she looked up at him with stricken eyes. 'That's why your call came as such a shock. I never thought for a moment that you would be in any danger in Madrid . . .'

'And when you found out,' Reade said bitterly, 'you left the sinking ship in a hell of a hurry.'

'That's hardly fair,' Georgia said. 'You told me someone had tried to kill you; someone was obviously willing to kill for that money, what else could it have been? I had to get out of Giz: what's the point of sitting like a target and waiting for it? You were relatively safe in Giz with the PIDE looking after you, but I wasn't . . . I chose you to go to Madrid because I wanted to cut you in . . . I thought it was safe . . .'

'Did you want to cut Frank in too?'

She shook her head impatiently. '*Frank* wanted to cut Frank in! The poor sod. He was moping around Giz and Lagos. He thought running a bloody Portuguese pub was going to be glamorous, and when he found it was mostly work, and no money, and if you were drunk and paid late you got fined, and you had to keep a clear head to get the paper work done . . . and the winter was miserable . . . My God, the only time you could even hold a conversation with the man was between six and seven in the evening; he was just getting over his last night's hangover and he wasn't drunk enough yet to tune out. *He* wanted in on this deal, friend. He wanted excitement, he wanted to play soldier. But he

164

kept saying it was for you, or for me, or for the Casabranca, or all three . . . But it was for himself, the . . . damn . . .'

She brushed some of the money off the bed in an enraged gesture.

'I wanted you,' she said. 'When I met you, I wanted you, and I wanted you in on it. I thought it was safe, but when he tried to kill you, I decided we should take this money for ourselves, all of it. I've made an arrangement with a Swiss who knows a lot about banking. He's meeting us at two this afternoon. I got his name and number from Frank, before he left for London. We weren't supposed to know it, but Frank found it out and gave it to me . . . just in case.' She smiled without pleasure. 'We're meeting in the park,' she said. 'Very cloak and dagger. He's wearing a blue suit and a white carnation and I'm wearing a red scarf.'

'Who is this guy?' He still stood in the centre of the room.

'What difference does that make?' she said. 'The less you know . . .'

'Is it the Cold Stove League?'

She nodded. 'After we split with him,' she said, 'we'll have a half million for ourselves. We go around the bastard who tried to kill you . . . if that's what he was doing in that alley.'

She looked straight in front of her, and said, 'You like to play games too, don't you?

165

You thought you could solve the whole problem with one great individual performance. You really got off on that, didn't you?'

Through Reade's rage he had a flash of his own vanity, his own foolishness. He had thought he was being enormously clever when he set out for Madrid. He sat down next to her on the bed, ignoring the money.

'Listen,' he said, 'maybe we should give the money back. The police will help us—'

She looked incredulous. 'You're joking,' she said.

'Well, this is no good, is it? I'm serious. You're compounding the original crime . . . whatever it was. You're stealing from a killer. We'll be running away from him for the rest of our lives, won't we?'

'No,' she said eagerly. 'No, we won't. Everything's set up: numbered bank accounts, papers, airline tickets. Our Swiss contact has done everything. We can start over . . .'

He leapt to his feet again, enraged.

'But what's wrong with you?' he shouted. 'Can't you hear me? People are dead, people have been killed. Let's get out of this! Leave the money here, right here, in this room. Send your Swiss friend a note and tell him to pick it up; he can have it. Let him fight with whoever wants it. The hell with the whole thing!'

He felt as though he were going to burst into tears. He was flooded with self-pity; he felt sorry for his own vulnerability, naïveté and bravado; for his self-delusion . . . He was the one who had sent Frank, wasn't he? And he felt sorry for Frank and he felt sorry for Georgia, who sat miserably on the bed, next to the money . . .

He sat down again, gently, and put his arm around her.

'I'm sorry,' he said, in a low voice. 'I just meant . . . the money isn't that important. I can sell the Casabranca, you know, I can go back to work in New York. I make—I made a lot of money; they still want me. I can take care of you. We don't need that money.'

'Oh,' Georgia said. 'Michael . . .'

They embraced, almost desperately. Their mouths were both hot and dry and they ground them together. Then the rustling of their bodies among the banknotes on the bed was broken into by the shrill, insistent piping of the telephone. Georgia stretched, snatching it from the cradle. She listened, nodded, then handed it to Reade.

'It's the front desk,' she said. 'You left your passport there.'

'Hello,' Reade said. The passport was in his pocket, but perhaps this call was from Silva . . .

It was Silva. 'I'm sorry to interrupt you,' he said, in his stilted English voice. 'It is

167

urgent that you meet me as soon as possible in the coffee shop on the fifth floor. It is a question of the lady's safety.'

'Of course,' Reade said. 'Right away.' He turned to Georgia, who sat looking at him. Her face was somewhat strained.

'I'll be right back,' he said. 'I have to go down there for a minute and get the passport.'

'Always something, isn't it?' she said. She smiled at him. 'Hurry back,' she said.

CHAPTER TWENTY-SIX

The elevator seemed to be moving especially slowly. Suddenly Reade yawned spasmodically. Nerves, he thought.

The doors opened directly on the bright, airy breakfast room. Only one table was occupied: three people sat in the corner. They looked like Americans: two men in short-sleeved white shirts and a woman in a dotted dress. A glass wall spanned the room. The view was spectacular: the orange and white hills and valleys of Lisbon, blurred by a rainy mist.

Reade wavered a moment, and then approached the group in the corner. There was no one else in sight.

'Excuse me,' he said, 'have you seen

168

someone up here—a Portuguese in a white suit? Or maybe a uniform? He wears glasses.'

The Americans looked at one another.

One of the men shook his head, then went on with the conversation. He had a southern drawl:

'Ya give a fella tenure and he don't cut the mustard, whatya gonna do?'

'He was supposed to be *dedicated* to scholarship,' added the woman across the table in a nasal whine. 'Restoration Comedy.'

It had begun to dawn on Reade that perhaps he had been tricked. He so intensely wanted it not to be that he was momentarily tongue-tied. He rolled his eyes, trying to regain the attention of his academic countrymen.

'They's no evidence he ever even finished his dissertation,' the man declared with indignation. The second man was backed into the corner, looking like a trapped animal. Through the window, Reade could just make out the castle and the old Arab quarter on the opposite hill. The residential buildings just beneath them had TV aerials shaped like dollar signs.

'And just let me tell you what this old boy in the German Department did,' the woman began, but the peculiar reality of the vista brought Reade back out of his inertia. He put both palms on their table, rattling cups and saucers. The woman had begun to suck a yellow plum, as if to punctuate her sentence, but Reade's intrusion surprised her and juice ran down her chin as she looked up.

'You're absolutely *sure* no one was in this room. No one?'

'Not for forty five minutes anyways,' said the man in the corner, flourishing his watch in affirmation.

It had not been Silva on the phone at all. And Georgia was alone in the room with the money!

He went quickly to the elevator and pushed the button. After a moment he pushed it again. It was taking too long. He went down the corridor; there was a door with red letters over it: *Saida*. Exit. He scrambled down the steps three at a time.

He turned the knob to room 221 and went inside quickly, to find Georgia sprawled on the rug. He knelt over here. There was blood on her hair. She had been shot behind the ear. Her face was very white. He felt with shaking fingers for her pulse. Nothing.

The bag was gonc. The money was gone too, from thc bcd.

He went into the bathroom and ran the cold water, splashing it on his face.

He couldn't be found with this . . . corpse. He had to get out. He walked back into the bedroom and over to the window, and carefully pulled the curtain aside. The black Mercedes was still there. There were two men

170

standing near the door, talking. Neither one was Silva.

He went to the door to the corridor and looked out, fearfully. No one in sight. He opened the door wider. The elevator was standing there, the doors open. No one was in the hall . . .

He made his way to the service stairs; at the bottom was an open door leading to the lobby, and a heavy metal door with a horizontal bar across it. He touched the bar and the door opened, into an alley, which led from the back of the building into a side street. Within seconds, it seemed, he was in an open plaza; a broad short street descended from it directly into the Avenida da Libertade. It was there that he hoped to find out where the Cold Stove was.

CHAPTER TWENTY-SEVEN

In a bookstore in the Libertade he bought a green *Michelin Guide* and walked over the black and white checkered pavement, past nineteenth-century stone buildings which now held glass-fronted travel offices and oil companies, to a cafe where he sat down at an outdoor table and ordered a Fundador. He thought defiantly that it no longer mattered whether his brain rotted; things were falling to pieces around him.

He opened the *Michelin* and skimmed quickly through the section on the history of Lisbon. Proper nouns caught his eye—Tagus, Phoenician, Wellington—which had no significance for him. He began to read more slowly when he came to a section of maps and the Portuguese names of sites, translated into English on occasion.

He was sitting in the Praco dos Restauradores (no stars), just up the street from the Rossio (one star), the recommended starting point for tours of both medieval and Pombaline—eighteenth and nineteenth century—Lisbon. The Pombaline route went back through the Restauradores, up the Avenida da Libertade (one star), to the Praca Marques de Pombal (no stars). Pombal Square stood at the entrance to a large park, named after Edward VII of England, who had visited Lisbon in 1902. Inside the park, which was awarded one star, was an attraction which also merited one star:

THE COLD GREENHOUSE (ESTUFA FRIA).
Open 9 a.m. to 7 p.m. (6 p.m. in winter); admission: 2 esc. Wooden shutters in this cold greenhouse protect from the extremes of summer heat and winter cold the exotic plants which grow beside fishponds or cooling waterfalls near small grottoes.

Concerts of classical music are given in the garden during the high season.

Reade pushed aside his brandy glass and fanned himself with the *Guide*. Never mind 'Greenhouse'; the operative word was obviously 'estufa', which must have meant 'stove' to . . . to Frank? It sounded like the kind of thing Frank would come up with. In any case, the *Estufa Fria* obviously needed a visit.

Reade called the PIDE offices, but all he got was a taped voice, in Portuguese and English. He left a message for Silva. After he went into a shop and bought himself a red scarf he took a bus to Pombal Square: the bus creaked slowly up the Avenida, but not slowly enough. He got off in front of the Fenix Hotel with twenty minutes to spare. That is, there were twenty minutes to spare if Georgia had been telling the truth when she said there was going to be a meeting with the Swiss at two o'clock.

The Cold Stove or whatever it was, was on the left. Reade headed that way, jogging around the square, past the statue of the bewigged marquis and his straining horses; he could see the gardens of Edward VII's park.

Suddenly someone grabbed his arm. He came to a startled halt, almost losing his balance. It was an unshaven man in a chocolate-coloured suit. With an ingratiating

173

smile, he took a suéde box from his pocket.

'You *Ingles*?' he asked.

Reade shook his head.

'*Contrabando*,' the man said excitedly. 'Swiss watch, cheap.'

Reade shook his head again, and began to move away.

'Wholesale,' the man shouted after him. 'Swiss. I got more than one.'

Reade darted through the traffic to a tree-shaded walk on the periphery of the park, where he was assailed by three more watch salesmen, teenagers this time. Sidestepping them, he walked into an old man holding still another watch. 'Gold,' the old man cried mournfully after him.

Suddenly the air was sweet; clusters of trumpet-shaped purple flowers hung from the trees. A black arrow on a white sign pointed to the right. *Estufa Fria* was printed in white letters on the arrow. Reade quickened his pace, following the path, which wound downward, past a duck pond. A flamingo stood on one leg in the middle of an island in the pond. He passed under a gateway, marked by a sign: *Estufa Fria*. An old porter in an engineer's cap took two escudos from Reade who tied the red scarf around his neck. It was five minutes to two.

The *Estufa Fria* was a natural lowland in the heart of the park: it was a rain forest of banana fronds, covered with porous canvas

174

and bamboo slats and planted with tropical vegetation, and was dotted with ponds on which lily pads floated. Reade chose the largest of the five or six paths which led from the entranceway, and strode quickly on his way.

The flowers were marked with their names in Latin and Portuguese. He passed a giant toadstool, a pond filled with golden carp and a stone chimney studded with pink puffy flowers. The place was dimly lighted; there was a strobe effect when breezes rippled the bamboo slats. Fireflies, or something like them, flashed in the air, and the perfume was overpowering. There were walls of ferns, leaves the size of elephant's ears, and pillars of rock descending into deep black pools. There was no one about.

He crossed a broad unpaved avenue, and then a stone bridge over a swamp. Suddenly he was in a clearing: a large marble-and-glass building was cut out of the rock and jungle. He moved quickly behind the shelter of a tree. What sounded like the overture to *William Tell* resounded through the clearing. It was a green dream world; only the sounds of diesel engines from the city could still be heard faintly through the music.

He decided to climb a stone path winding off to his left, hoping that he might find a secure niche there from which he could observe this jungle. The climb was precarious, since the path was narrow and slippery. Water was dripping from an ordinary garden hose up near the bamboo ceiling, and trickling picturesquely over the rocks. As Reade climbed, the music faded away, and stopped.

He emerged directly above the bridge over the swamp, looking down on the broad dirt road which bisected the greenhouse, and a network of pathways, like an aimless vine. Suddenly he saw someone emerge from this network and cross the bridge. The man, wearing a blue suit and with a white flower in his buttonhole, hesitated, and then turned back over the bridge again, and stood on a flat, wide stone in the swamp, next to a rocky pillar which was encircled by the roots of a giant palmetto.

The man looked up and saw Reade. Their eyes met, and the man gestured imperiously, pointing to the bridge. Reade stood staring at him. The man gestured again, insistently, and Reade made his way carefully down a series of stone footholds which led to a natural archway of banana fronds on the far side of the bridge. It occurred to him that his life was probably in danger, and he wondered what in the world he was doing there. He missed his footing, felt water seep into his shoe, and then stepped onto solid ground. He was standing in a natural cave, protected by fern and elephant-ear. About four feet in front of him stood the man in the blue suit, a squat man, balding, with a square face—the light flashed from his eyeglasses.

'Who are you?' the man said in English. 'What about the woman?'

A jet whined loudly overhead; Reade saw his lips moving but he could not hear him. A red-fringed hole appeared suddenly in the man's white shirt, and he collapsed backward into a heap on the path. Reade instinctively moved toward him, and then dived under a cluster of immense leaves. He hunched there, absolutely still.

He could just as easily be Frank Driscoll. He had slept with Georgia, as Frank had. And he had slept in Frank's bed. He had tried to get away with something, as Frank had. And now, like Frank, he was going to be killed.

He tried to make himself smaller in his hiding place. Portugal, he thought, the land of port wine and bloodless bullfights . . .

His right leg cramped; he peeked from behind the leaf and saw Clive Mowbray wearing a safari jacket, training a rifle in his direction from the stone walkway some 50 yards above and to his left. There was an explosion and he felt a sudden searing pain above his ear. Then nothing.

CHAPTER TWENTY-EIGHT

In the windowless flat supplied to Browne by the U.S. Consulate, Michael Reade sat immobile in a large upholstered wing chair. His face was ashen except for a spot of red high in each cheek. The plaster over his ear added an aspect of encephalic deformity to the sickly pallor.

On a side-table next to the chair was a highball glass and a small bowl full of pink-and-grey capsules.

Across the room, Turner Cromwell sprawled on a sofa in a silk paisley dressing-gown, his thick, hairy calves exposed, as he ate sugar plums from Elvas.

Intermittently, Sam Browne, who was hard at work on one of the phones in the next room, would look in and offer to replenish Reade's glass with Wild Turkey bourbon, or suggest another Darvon for his pain.

In the meantime, Cromwell explained the sequence of financial situations and events which had led to Mowbray killing Frank Driscoll, Luis Reyes, Georgia Ryan, and Hans Hauptmann.

'The only thing we couldn't figure . . . after we made the connection between Frank Driscoll's corpse and T.S. Eliot . . . was how a bartender could handle such a sophisticated telex job. Then when we identified Hauptmann, and talked to some informants in Zurich, it became clear: magnetic tape. Pure and simple. Hauptmann did a program. Driscoll plugged it in to the machine.'

Browne popped his head in: 'This Hauptmann was something else.'

'He still is,' offered Reade. 'He's dead.'

Cromwell laughed and continued his discourse on Hauptmann. 'The Forex man had often been in litigation with WC over their virtual monopoly of teletype equipment in Western Europe. Moreover, he had a philosophical hatred for the equipment itself: all teletype and computerized stuff was depersonalizing, thus accelerating the mechanization of human relationships. The Big Three Swiss banks were his particular *bêtes noires* in this regard, and he liked to brag about getting rich at their expense.'

Cromwell huffed and puffed on his cigar, warming to the task. 'Now, you may say, "That's crazy, because the guy used teletype and exploited all the equipment and markets the other guys did." In fact, he used his expertise in these very areas to pull off the robbery, which he apparently saw as an act of revenge against the banks rather than as a way to make a profit. There are lots of other contradictions too. But he was crazy like a fox . . . tricky and obsessive. Ha ha. He just didn't do as well choosing people as he did manipulating machines. That's the best irony.'

Then Cromwell put out the cigarillo and munched candy with particular relish as he recounted the background of Mowbray, who had mishandled his own inheritance and then a substantial portion of his wife's, in at least three countries. Coincident with his mounting losses came his involvement with the Emergency Colonial Relief Fund, an extreme right-wing organization dedicated to, among other things, resisting the granting of independence to African nations. Now it appeared Mowbray had doublecrossed the Relief Fund people, as he had deceived his wife. In any case, there was no trace of him in Giz or Madrid. He had taken the money and run.

Cromwell poured more Wild Turkey into Reade's glass, and then dropped into it a couple of ice cubes from the styrofoam bucket which sat next to the sugar plums on the coffee table. 'There's a lot, of course, that we *don't* know,' said Cromwell. 'You've cleared up a few points, but we still don't know how Hauptmann and Mowbray got together. We can only guess that Reyes was an old Relief Fund contact. And, of course, we don't know why Mowbray killed Driscoll. Or how. Or what his relationship with the Ryan woman was. Why did she recruit you? Was it with Mowbray's knowledge? Obviously, at some

180

point communications broke down between them. If he was going to kill you all and take the money, why didn't he do it at once and be done with it?'

Browne looked in the door. He wore a short-sleeved wash-and-wear shirt with a striped tie, dacron slacks, and black military shoes. 'Colonel Cabral just called,' he said. 'He reports that Mowbray has still not been found, that your girlfriend,' he nodded to Reade, 'is being temporarily listed as a suicide, and Hauptmann as a missing person, to give us time to clear this up. He knows it will blow up in his face when the newshounds get hold of it,' he sighed deeply. 'He also advises us not to do a fucking thing within the borders of Portugal without his permission. If we do, he threatens an official diplomatic protest.'

Cromwell swung his hairy legs over and sat upright facing the other two men. He picked up a pencil and rapped it on the table.

'Screw him. We're legitimately protecting American investments. It's part of your agency's charter, and part of all the treaties anyway. Besides, Mowbray isn't in Portugal anymore. I'll bet on it. But where could he go? Michael, I'm afraid we're going to have to ask you some more questions.'

Reade nodded resentfully without making a sound. He popped one of the Darvons into his mouth and washed it down with a large

181

slug of whisky.

Cromwell lighted a narrow cigar and waved it about like a baton.

'Hold on!' The cigar made smoke rings over Cromwell's shiny pate. 'I've just put my finger on *the* question that we forgot to ask.' He grinned evilly, mouth hanging open. His teeth were so straight, and of such an unnatural oatmeal colour that they had to be false.

'Yes, Turner?' asked Browne.

'It's about currency. It was Mowbray, not Hauptmann, who gave Reyes his orders at the Madrid end of the transaction, right? Yet we never bothered to find out what kind of money the crippled patriot ultimately turned it into.'

'Wrong,' bellowed Browne. 'Silva told us, remember. And we had the chauffeur peek in the back of the Volksy at the border to make sure that Reade was carrying more than he was showing. It was pesetas.'

'But Silva only counted what Reade showed him. And the chauffeur only looked in the top of the package. So Reade is the only one who's seen the entire bundle. Reade?'

During this exchange. Reade had looked vaguely at the wall, sipping his drink. He did not respond immediately to Cromwell's question.

'Reade!' screamed Browne, ecstatic with the noise of discovery.

Reade buried his nose in the glass until the ice cubes fell and bumped against his teeth.

'Pesetas and francs,' he said into the glass. 'Half and half.'

'What kind of francs?' asked Cromwell, leaning intently across the styrofoam bucket. 'French or Swiss?'

'French,' mumbled Reade. 'French.'

Cromwell stood and paced about the room, trailing the silk gown. Browne's hands were interlocked at his belt buckle; he appeared to be doing isometric exercises. Veins stood out on his neck.

'French francs and pesetas,' Cromwell muttered for the tenth time. Suddenly, he snapped his fingers, walked into the next room, and dialled the phone. 'Come in here, will you Sam?' he called. Browne closed the door behind him.

Reade sat in silence as the voices of Cromwell and Browne, indistinct, filtered through the door. Then there was a sequence of telephone calls. Once Reade rose, walked creakily to the bottle, filled his glass without bothering with ice, and fell back into the chair.

After half an hour, the two men returned. Cromwell's pink cheeks were wreathed in smiles.

'What's the one place in the world where French and Spanish currencies are used interchangeably? A smugglers' paradise where a thief and scoundrel like Mowbray can hope to live to a prosperous old age, no questions asked, no passports required?

'I'll tell you where,' he answered his own question after suitable pause. '*Andorra!* Where else?'

'The WC Lear is gassing up,' said Browne. 'But first, Michael Reade, my boy, Cromwell and I are going to write a scenario. And you better learn your part *good*!'

CHAPTER TWENTY-NINE

The Citroën entered an ancient village, far removed from the strips of conspicuous consumption which were the towns of Les Escaldes and Andorre-le-Vieille, whose main streets bore miles of signs and window displays competing for the pedestrian's attention: PHONOS, GIRARD, REMY-MARTIN, CAVA, TABAC, TRANSISTORS, JOHNNY WALKER, CASHMERE, SEIKO, SONY, PERFUMERIA, BLAUPUNKT, OMEGA, DUTY FREE, DUTY FREE, DUTY FREE . . . In the village the streets were lined with tall trees and there were no construction cranes or concrete mixers which had given the other Andorran towns a brash Southern Californian look.

A policeman in a white helmet with a chinstrap, wearing a burgundy jacket with a gold sunburst badge, and black trousers with a white stripe, held up his baton and halted the car. A funeral procession emerged from a flat-fronted stone church. One of the pallbearers was wearing a brown suit and blue sneakers. Another mourner was carrying brass candlesticks. A bell tolled. A man with a loaf of bread under his arm cut through the procession. Browne said something to the driver in Spanish, then he turned to Reade.

'Okay,' he said. 'Here's the hotel. This is where you get off.'

They had come in from the French side at Cromwell's insistence. The border was less sensitive, the airports were closer, and the food was superior. So the closed car was permeated with the odour of garlicky preserved goose and Armagnac, the residuum of their brief luncheon sojourn at an *auberge* in the foothills between Foix and Ax-les-Thermes. Reade had begun to feel claustrophobic, and was almost relieved to step into the fresh air.

Almost.

CHAPTER THIRTY

Reade rose late, skipped breakfast and stepped across the road to the cafe at the telecabin lift which carried passengers to the scenic area of the Lac d'Engolasters. This had become his custom in the five days which he had spent in Andorra. Two bodyguards, disguised as French fishermen, watched him from the terrace of the hotel . . . the third one at which he had stayed, asking provocative questions about newcomers from Portugal. Browne and Cromwell were staying in Les Escaldes where there was a swimming pool.

Reade sat down and ordered Spanish Fundador and coffee. He watched the compact red cars circle the motor housing, lurch back onto the twin cables and climb slowly out of sight. The counterman was garrulous and full of complaints: there was not enough business, he said, it was foolish to open the lift before July, and in any case the man in charge of the base, he himself, should also be in control of the cablecars. It was a waste of energy to have them in motion on a dull day like today. The proprietor of the restaurant at the lake, a cousin of the owner, controlled the lift; he shut off the *teleferique* frequently at mealtimes so that passengers were trapped at his restaurant and consequently forced to eat there. Today only one family, a group of Swedes, had taken the cars, carrying a picnic lunch. It was a shame: one family.

Reade nodded agreement. He took some French francs from his pocket and put them on the bar, ordering another Domecq. Life seemed to be conspiring to make him an alcoholic. Drinking in the morning. One of the red modules came down, hitting the platform with a shudder. The empty car opened its doors, whipped around and pointed itself back toward the mountain and came to a shivering stop. The door slid open again.

'Oh, Michael,' a voice said.

Reade looked up inquiringly. Clive Mowbray was poised in the door of the two-man car, and beckoning.

'Would you step over here,' he said. His coat was draped oddly over his shoulders. The sun glinted on a gun barrel.

Reade got up and walked to the lift.

'If you would just get in,' Mowbray said. 'I'd just as soon not attract anybody's attention.'

The two French fishermen on the hotel terrace were playing cards and glancing in his direction. Reade got into the car and fell back into the snug seat. Mowbray, despite his bulk, entered rather gracefully. They sat facing each other, knee to knee. The door slid to a close. Grinding noisily, the cablecar swung aloft, swaying on its steel wire. Reade's back was to the mountain; he could see his bodyguards receding below him.

'Now that's quite comfy, isn't it?' Mowbray said. 'I take it you've been looking for me.'

'What makes you think so?' Reade said.

Mowbray looked at him. 'I think you should not attempt to play the fool,' he said, mildly. 'You aren't quite that bad, you know, old chap. I'd really like to know whom you represent. It's not your friend Silva, surely? Perhaps one of the banks?'

'That guy you shot in the park,' Reade said. 'He kept saying something about Andorra before he died. I was only winged by that bullet, you know, and when I got better I decided to try to follow the money . . .'

'Now, now,' Mowbray said. 'Really. They just let you go? After all that mess? But Michael, really, I didn't take Hans into my confidence. I can't see him maundering about Andorra in a deathbed statement, unless he had decided to come here too through an extraordinary coincidence . . . I really think you're telling me a lie. And those two gorillas watching you from the hotel. This is the last car that will go up the mountain for an hour, you know. The manager of the restaurant has closed the lift . . . my suggestion, of course.'

They were far above the valley now; the

188

hotel and the base lodge had merged with the small cluster of houses that comprised Encamp into a smudge of grey in a larger pattern of brown fields, green meadows and yellow gardens, enclosed by the white forbidding peaks of the Pyrenees. The telecabin rocked in the wind.

'I'd really like to know why you came here,' Mowbray said. 'It would take a load off my mind, old chap. Obviously you were looking for me. What could you possibly hope to gain? I mean, you've found me, haven't you?'

'The money,' Reade said. 'It's always the money, isn't it? I thought we could work out a deal. I mean, I saw you in the park . . .'

'Ah, did you? Unfortunately for you . . .'

'I saw you,' Reade repeated. 'And the money . . . D'you think I didn't notice, half Spanish and half French? That meant Andorra.'

'Well, that's incredibly astute of you, old fellow. I really didn't think you had it in you. And you kept all this to yourself, did you? No one helped you to draw conclusions?'

Reade tried to think clearly. If Mowbray knew about Browne and Cromwell, would that help Reade or hurt him? And there were those 'fishermen' on the balcony . . .

'Well,' Reade said slowly, 'there were some people from the banks. I will admit they talked to me about all this.'

'And you told them you saw me . . .'
Reade paused.

Without warning Mowbray kicked him in the shin with his steel-toed boot.

'I asked you a question,' he said pleasantly.

Reade's eyes were filled with tears of pain and rage.

'Yes,' he said. 'I told them about you.'

Mowbray kicked him again.

'I think you're lying,' he said, 'you disgusting little toad. I don't think you saw me in the park at all. I don't think the penny dropped until a few moments ago, in the cafe, and I don't think you told your friends about me.' He leaned forward, until his flushed, puffy face was very close to Reade's. 'What do you think of that?' he said.

Reade was hunched over, his hands closed protectively around his leg.

'If you kick me again,' he said thickly, 'I won't be able to walk. What do you think of that?'

Mowbray laughed, a natural laugh. 'Very good,' he said. 'I'll try another place then, shall I? Your face, for instance, which I gather is your fortune. Or,' he said, leaning forward again, 'I could simply pitch you out of here and be done with it. I'd just as soon they didn't find you strewn about the landscape, though. Ah, too late anyway. Here we are.'

CHAPTER THIRTY-ONE

'Have a seat,' Mowbray said. 'I think you're a little out of condition.'

Reade sank gratefully onto the damp ground. Mowbray perched on a large rock, and lighted a cigarette deftly with one hand. The tall evergreens around them swayed in the wind. From the clearing where they sat, Reade could see a large meadow, and beyond that what looked like a blue lake.

'We have some time,' Mowbray said. 'I don't want to tire you.'

'You're terribly clever,' Reade said. 'Awfully witty. For a man who decided to rely on Frank Driscoll.'

Mowbray smiled. 'I could say the same to you, old man,' he said. 'Well, I mean after all he was available. He wasn't essential anyway. No, the clever thing I did, you see, was to meet Hauptmann. Now *he* was the one with the ideas, and with the connections: bought a man at Crédit Suisse, and knew this fellow Anderson at Lloyds.' The wind lifted the wings of his colourless hair. 'But think,' he said dreamily, puffing at the cigarette, 'think how convenient old Frank was. Not bright, needed escudos, and had a business we could launder some money through. And looking for thrills, wasn't he, a bit of a flop at

191

everything he did . . .'

He ground out the cigarette on the boulder and stood up.

'Let's get going,' he said.

Reade rose with some difficulty. The pain in his leg was agonizing. The rage he felt was tying his stomach in knots. He limped along, with Mowbray slightly behind him.

'Yes, your friend was a flop,' Mowbray said. 'A drunk. A fool. A clown.' He seemed to get a good deal of pleasure out of saying these things.

'And that stupid woman,' he went on, 'that stupid greedy woman. She and Frank together, a convenient pair. Oh, I know all that talk about me; living on my wife, that sort of talk. And all the time I was laughing at them, laughing all the way to the bank, so to speak.'

'Georgia,' Reade began. He tripped suddenly over a root and fell to his knees. The pain was so intense that for a moment he thought he was going to throw up.

'Get up,' Mowbray said, through his teeth. 'Get up, get up, you imbecile, you fucking idiot.'

He raised his pistol and brought it down forcibly across the base of Reade's spine. 'Get *up*,' he said.

Reade scrambled to his feet, trembling violently. He had bitten his lip; he could feel blood running down his chin.

'Do watch your step,' Mowbray said, in a normal voice. 'You were saying? Georgia? I hope you didn't take her too seriously, old man. They were going to deport her as a disorderly person, you know; her husband complained about her, poor man.'

They walked in silence, their pace very slow.

'She knew about you,' Reade said. The words were bitter in his mouth, mixed with blood.

'Oh, she definitely knew about me,' Mowbray said, with enjoyment. 'I quite see that she did not share that knowledge with you. I simply told her that Frank had gotten greedy and wanted more money. He tried to blackmail me in a meeting at Sagres. Well, she understood, of course. She couldn't have been more sympathetic, old boy. She offered to find Frank's bag with the tapes for me. I'd already found it, of course, but I let her look anyway. She decided to bring you in as Frank's replacement—you were something of a shock altogether. Frank had neglected to mention that you owned the business. He wasn't trustworthy at all.'

'Frank blackmailed you,' Reade said.

Mowbray laughed again, a natural lilting laugh. 'Oh, you idiot,' he said. 'I told her that. It was my little story. No,' he said ruminatively, 'I didn't really need Frank after all, did I? He made the most awful balls-up in

193

London; our friend Hauptmann had a fit. I mean, I don't object to a bit of drama. I enjoy it myself; I wore this ghastly wig, you know, and met Anderson . . . But Frank was a drunk, and that's dangerous.'

They had reached the gravelly shore of the lake, and Mowbray stopped there, and reflectively kicked some small stones into the water.

'I knew he was dangerous early on,' he said. 'And I think I handled it very well. I had Reyes give me the proper currencies . . . It was a shame, really: there was supposed to be a Levant, Frank was supposed to wash out to sea. But the wind changed, I'm afraid, and then Frank was naturally buoyant, wasn't he? But I won't rely on wind shifts with you.'

He prodded Reade hard with the gun and they began to move again, faster. Reade was limping. A path had opened up; it moved along the shoreline to what looked like a big dam ahead.

'Frank was the sort who goes to seed in the tropics,' Mowbray said. 'I had years in Singapore, you know. I'm used to outposts. You'd go to seed here too,' he said. 'You and that whore. She was going to cut me out; she made her own arrangements with Hauptmann. But what a fool!'

The sound of water was mixed with the drone of generators.

'In a few minutes,' he said in a

conversational tone, 'they will open the sluice gates of the dam, and I'm going to shove you in there. You will be sucked through the gates into the turbine which powers the generator, and when you're spewed out of that, into the network of canals that irrigates this valley, you'll be all slivers and shreds—spread throughout the principality, like fertilizer, which I find a rather apt simile.'

'Wait a minute,' Reade cried. 'Look, I've got money, some of your money . . .'

He pulled from his pocket the bearer's note he had found in Frank's flat eons ago, and held it out.

Mowbray moved closer to look at it. 'Well,' he said, 'I won't say I'm unhappy to get it . . .'

At this point he heard the helicopter. He stiffened, and Reade pushed him quickly off balance, drew back, and then plunged his head hard into the Englishman's stomach, before he could raise the Webley. Mowbray grunted; he was very strong. The pistol thudded on the ground. Mowbray kicked out with his steel-toed boot, but Reade avoided it, twisting around behind Mowbray and catching up his foot. The Englishman fell heavily, and Reade held on; they rolled together to the edge of the water, near the dam wall.

A loud voice called 'STOP! STOP!' It was

coming from the helicopter.

Reade relaxed suddenly. Mowbray, as if by reflex, followed suit. It was an old football trick. As Mowbray's grip loosened subtly, Reade gathered what strength he had left into his arms and hands: he flipped Mowbray over by the bunched corduroy of his jacket with one hand, held fast to his wrist with the other, and snapped the arm at the elbow.

A scream burst from Mowbray's lips. Reade, exhausted, relaxed again, and his adversary stumbled somehow up the slight incline and onto the dam itself. Reade was aware that Browne and Cromwell and some other men were running toward them across the stonework, calling out. Their voices were drowned in the roar when the sluice gates opened.

From a crouch, Reade charged up the incline. Mowbray was holding a large rock; he brought it down viciously on Reade's shoulder. The pain called up a demented rage: Reade struck out with his right fist. Mowbray teetered for a moment over the flood. The water thundered; Reade struck him again, above the ear, this time, and Mowbray hurtled downward, and disappeared into the foamy turbulence. He resurfaced at the lip of the gate, holding onto the cement with his good arm. The face which had so often swallowed itself in laughter looked wide open, the features

196

stretched, the hair, which had been colourless wings, dark and flat against his head.

The bearer's note was lying crumpled on the gravel. Reade climbed painfully down from the dam, and picked it up and put it in his pocket. Mustn't trifle with liquid assets, he thought, liquid assets, pretty funny, and then Mowbray lost his grip and was sucked silently under the white water.

Browne was at his side, and Cromwell was almost hopping up and down in fury.

'Look what you've done,' he said, 'You asshole. Didn't we tell you we wanted him? You've lost the money!'

Browne shook his head. 'Amateurs,' he said, 'can't you get anything straight? You've killed him. He's dead, and he wasn't supposed to die. That wasn't in the scenario; you were only supposed to be the decoy, the still!'

Reade turned his head slowly to look at them. The sun burned down from a cloudless sky; his shoulder felt as though it were broken, and his leg was wobbling beneath him.

'I was misinformed,' he said.

Photoset, printed and bound in Great Britain by REDWOOD BURN LIMITED, Trowbridge, Wiltshire